BOOKS BY JOSEPH HELLER

Portrait of an Artist, as an Old Man

Joseph Heller

Scribner Paperback Fiction
Published by Simon & Schuster
New York London Toronto Sydney Singapore

SCRIBNER PAPERBACK FICTION
Simon & Schuster, Inc.
Rockefeller Center
1230 Avenue of the Americas
New York, NY 10020

First Scribner Paperback Fiction edition 2001

SCRIBNER PAPERBACK FICTION and design are trademarks of Macmillan Library Reference USA, Inc., used under license by Simon & Schuster, the publisher of this work.

Designed by Ellen R. Sasahara

Manufactured in the United States of America
10 9 8 7 6 5 4 3 2 1

Library of Congress Cataloging-in-Publication Data is available.

ISBN 0-7432-0200-7
0-7432-0201-5 (Pbk)

Portrait of

an Artist,

as an Old

Man

TOM

"Tom."

No answer.

"Tom."

Still no answer.

"Oh, shit," said Aunt Polly. "Where in the world can that boy be this time, I wonder?"

That boy, Tom Sawyer, was lounging in an armchair up front in the parlor in his new Armani cashmere sport jacket, complacently calculating the overnight appreciation of his stock and bond holdings as he waited for four of his friends to come by in the leased stretch limousine with insolent smoked windows to take them all to the luxury box in the stadium for the big game—football or basketball, he had forgotten which, perhaps a prizefight. It did not matter to him. What mattered was that he be there. He had bedecked himself in a Turnbull & Asser shirt of aubergine vertical stripes with a gleaming white collar, unbuttoned at the neck. His suspenders were wide and of a red-and-black polka dot. Proudly and deceptively, he had already devised a tricky new riddle to entrap his gullible pals once more into bets of $300 each they were sure they'd win and were certain to lose. He would entice them at the start with an idle observation, as though thinking out loud, the vague surmise "You know, it really is hard for me to accept the fact that—"

Oh, shit, sighed the elderly author with great regret, and decided to give up on this book too.

Listlessly, he rolled the ballpoint pen away. The last thing he wanted to do now, he told himself, was tax his brain to devise a convincing crafty riddle for the expectations raised in the text in order to move it along; the one he'd had in mind for a start he'd already used before as a bit in an earlier novel, that Reno, Nevada, and Spokane, Washington, were both farther west than Los Angeles. No one might catch the repetition. But *he* would know, and that single cheat could be enough to engender self-contempt, and then induce him to loaf along in other areas too. It was not worth the effort, he sensed already. This book-length parody of the quintessential American pop novel *Tom Sawyer*, with a contemporary Tom Sawyer and a law degree from Yale or a master's degree in business administration from Harvard, was definitely not going to forge in the smithy of his soul the uncreated conscience of the world, or his race, whichever. Not now, he reflected with a rueful smile, certainly not this one in what he had already begun thinking of privately, with dismaying irony, as this last portrait in literary form by the artist as an old man. Although that, as always, was never for a minute what he seriously had in mind. And not even James Joyce had succeeded in making that long stretch to metaphysical perfection in his *Portrait of the Artist as a Young Man*. But this latest gambit, he now judged, was simple, hackneyed satire, affording no space for expanded aesthetic experimentation or for ambivalent domestic conflicts or wrenching tragedies, and of a kind that swarms of gifted newspaper and magazine writers could do in half a day with eight hundred words, while he would need three or four years for his novel and fill four hundred pages.

A lifetime of experience had trained him never to toss away a page he had written, no matter how clumsy, until he had gone over it again for improvement, or had at least stored it in a folder for safekeeping or recorded the words on his computer.

About this one he had no second thoughts. Oh, shit, he softly repeated, murmuring out loud this time, and gently removed the top sheets from his lined yellow pad and crumpled them into his wicker wastebasket. He overcame the urge to lie down for a second morning nap. Sighing again, he reached for a cardigan sweater and scarf and stepped outside his study for a walk to the beach that he hoped might clear his head and leave him wider awake with more mental celerity than he presently commanded. As he shuffled down his driveway in an overtired walk, he spied his wife across the lawn, regarding him from a corner of the house beside a large garden bucket, clutching a watering can with both her hands. He did not need to peer closely to know that her expression would be that familiar one of sympathy and disappointment at this evidence of failure of his newest daily attempt, and perhaps with the momentary disdain that he was experiencing for himself. Her name was Polly—Polly too; the recurrence in feminine name of the one he had just played with on paper dawned on him for the first time, and then only as a light coincidence. He waved limply, with no emotion, as he passed, forcing something of a smile, and quickened his step until he was at the bottom of the driveway and had turned out of sight on the road. Then he lapsed back into his torpid stroll, almost with a shimmer of relief to consider himself unobserved.

Thirty-five minutes went by before he reached the beach. He was not in a hurry. He heard himself breathing heavily when he arrived, but not excessively so, he hoped, for a man of his years. The wooden bench on which he seated himself to rest was empty. He gazed with intentionally cleared mind at the peaceful scene of sand and water and vacant horizon, waiting for something marvelous to occur to him. He examined with blank eyes the several distant people sauntering along the shore, some with unleashed dogs. Most were women—he was conscious these days that his attention fixed on the appearance of women more and more often, more than ever before since they started wearing tight-fitting trousers of one sort or another with the outline of their underpants explicitly traced, and miniskirts too—and these women seemed perceptibly shorter and more heavyset than normal as they trudged along flat-footed through the sand. He seldom noted what men looked like, or cared.

Where, he wondered, had ingenuity gone? He could guess some answers, for himself and for so many of his contemporaries, and for renowned others of similar occupation who now were long gone. In earlier days of youthful mental vigor and stronger drive the dependable literary thoughts and inspirations that vaulted out of nowhere into mind whenever he beckoned for them had seemed inexhaustible. Now he had to ponder and wait. Pondering and waiting, he stared dully at the unfettered flocks of birds in view, the gulls and terns gliding overhead, the sandpipers scurrying along the shore for their meal of worms as the last splashes of surf were sucked back into the sea. He craved almost desperately for the flicker of a vibrant and usable idea to come gliding into his attention from somewhere in an illuminating flash of revelation, from anywhere, like a bird, a beautiful, glittering bird spontaneously on its own, as never had failed to grace him in his more prolific past, an idea fertile with throbbing possibilities that would revitalize the imagination and invigorate his spirit. His mind wandered. His eyes glazed. His head felt heavy and started to droop. He let his lids slither closed. He might even have dozed. He came awake slowly, thinking, his lips moving in a dialogue, and straightened alertly with the feeling his prayers mystically had been answered. He stood up with a start.

His walk back was close to ten minutes quicker. He made directly toward the low wooden building that served as his studio and as sleeping quarters for overnight guests on the rare occasions they invited any. He was breathing more heavily than earlier but paid no attention. Polly, working now with rose clippers and studying him intently, took notice of his brisker walk and purposeful attitude. She smiled appreciatively and responded to his jaunty wave with a beaming reciprocity of delight and optimism. He was perspiring a bit. Inside, he speedily rinsed the body moisture from his neck and face with splashes of cold water from the sink in the bathroom and then hurried to his swivel chair at the desk. Switching his radio on, he took hold of his yellow pad and ballpoint pen. He was aware only dimly that he had been humming the melody to the Caribbean song called "Yellow Bird" until the music welled through on the classical station to which the radio was always tuned. It was by pure good luck the exuberant last movement of the popular Haydn cello concerto. An omen. He was elated.

YELLOW BIRD

"It won't sing."

"It's dead."

The young boy, Irv, had figured that much out for himself but did not want the saleswoman in the pet shop of the department store to suspect he knew. And Irv certainly did not want anyone in his family to guess he had allowed the new canary out of the cage, to see, in suspense, what it would do. He had lowered the windows and shut the door. What the canary did when released, after peeking peckishly right and left, was fly headfirst into the mirror over the dresser, drop, and lie still, discharging a slight shudder of feathers as it drew its last breath.

"My mother wants her money back," Irv lied, looking guileless and ignorant. "She has a charge account here."

Years later, he remembered the yellow bird and labeled the experience his first brush with death. Also his first advantageous negotiation. His first constructive deception. It was all so easily fruitful he resolved to try dishonesty again whenever a situation counseled chicanery. Like Tom Sawyer, he was fond of mischievous deceit, and his antics had never, until the present, tumbled him into trouble. Foppishly, he'd felt himself invulnerable. Absurdly, when elected to the presidency of the country, he'd chosen for himself the code name Yellowbird.

"What happened to the canary?" his mother had asked at home that evening. "Where's the cage?"

Irv saw no recourse but to make a clean breast of it. "It wouldn't sing," he answered. "I brought them back to the store. I got you a credit."

"It sang yesterday," said his brother, who was older.

"It wouldn't sing today."

"Why wouldn't they give you one that does sing?"

"They didn't have any left."

"Why didn't you give it another day?"

"It was dead," said Irv.

"Dead?"

"That's what they said."

"Like the dog in the car," snickered his brother. "When you locked him in and forgot you put him there."

"The dog didn't die," objected his sister, who enjoyed contradicting her brother.

"No, because I was the only one in the family who noticed he wasn't around and asked."

Forty-five years later, when holed up quaking in the White House as though in an imperiled stronghold, and confronted by the impending ignominious dishonor of impeachment, he recalled this childhood exploit with the canary, and in his next lamebrained and squirming, sorrowful, insincere, apologetic speech he impetuously injected a line of poetry he'd come upon far back in a place he no longer remembered by a poet no longer of importance to him, interpolating, "I would rather learn from one bird how to sing than teach ten thousand stars how not to shine . . . or dance." That sounded great, he thought, and infused with an ardent surge of confidence, he hastened to venture further into the domain of arts and letters and raced on extemporaneously with a line he associated with Eleanor Roosevelt, that, to wit, it was better to light a candle than curse the darkness. He was pleased with himself after that one too and was basking in his own scholarly sense of himself even before he finished.

His speechwriters and closest advisers, on the other hand, were aghast. In shocked states of agonized helplessness, they glared at each other with outrage. "That *putz!*" grumbled the one from New York City. "That very dumb *putz!*" Another, with a polite growl of apology, stepped outside to vomit.

"For someone who is thought of as a smart politician," muttered Irv's wife, who was watching him on television in another room, "your father is often pretty stupid, isn't he?"

"I think I've already noticed that," agreed his teenage daughter.

Airily, Irv later waved aside their frowns and other agitated disclosures of disapproval. He knew he could count on all in his family to stand by him through the harrowing times ahead. Fortunately, he had no family fortune. For the time being, they had no better place to go, no better place to live than in the White House. But unfortunately also, he had no family fortune, and he too had no better place than the White House in which to live for the next couple of years, albeit on a salary absurdly small for the amount of work expected of him and the intense pressure of demands and public reassessment focused always upon all of them. If he could manage to hang on for just another two years, though, he'd be retired with something of a pension and something of an aura of respectability. Actually, he had half a mind to let go now and resign in leisurely disgrace, once assured the disgrace to him would be no more damaging or lasting than it had been to predecessors among other political reprobates in Washington, and once assured of a decent place to live and a lifetime income enabling him to take things easy and once in a while chew the fat at state funerals with the clutch of other living ex-presidents who regularly turned up, dull though they might be, as dull and hollow, certainly, as he himself. He was between a rock and a hard place—he might use that one too the next time he had to face the public—but Irv had no doubt that, as he was fond of repeating, when the going got tough, the tough got going, and that in the end, when between a rock and a hard place, he and truth, noble truth would—

Oh, shit, for heaven's sake! And the hell with that one too, he decided.

Who cared? What could it lead to that was worthwhile? Another political farce, another dysfunctional family yarn? Any serious literary work treating those contaminated buffoons in Washington as a herd of contaminated buffoons could no longer be serious or even fresh or striking. It would have to be ludicrous and thin, anything *but* serious, and there had already been too many of those. No one of conscience who knew anything looked up to those dolts in office anymore or expected much. Moreover, he had the feeling—he *knew*—that he had already done that subject to smaller or larger extent in one earlier work of his or another. Profoundly discouraging to him in his present state was the woebegone feeling that everything he thought of writing about he had already written about before at least once in exactly that same vein. And reluctant to repeat himself, he did not know who else to strive to imitate.

Again he pushed his pad and pen away from him in a lazy motion that had become all but automatic, rose, and with a soughing noise he didn't hear, grimly stretched himself out atop the bed in his studio and closed his eyes. It used to be, when younger, he remembered, and in finer fettle, he would get some of his best ideas and nouns and adjectives while lying down that way—and, he snorted inwardly, some of his worst, like the one just now, and the one just before.

What next, then?

The artificer who lives long enough, particularly the writer of fictions for page and stage, may come to a time in his life when he feels he has nothing new to write about but wishes to continue anyway. Musicians joke in belittlement about the last compositions of Mozart, who died young, that he did not die soon enough. Shakespeare did know when to quit: "Our revels now are ended," he wrote in *The Tempest*, and departed with his winnings for the role of a country squire in Stratford in preference to the bacchanalian romps of theater life in London, for which, it can be safely inferred, he likely found he had grown too old. The man who could shrewdly observe when young that "liquor increases desire but weakens performance" would certainly recognize from personal debacles that the passage of years, with liquor or without, could weaken desire too, and, as well, reduce the compelling force of a lifelong theatrical ambition that had been largely and long fulfilled. Verdi was great with *Otello* even into his seventies, but Verdi was indeed a great one, and a great exception. Most of us flag with age, and with experience too. The work gets no easier with practice, and when we stop, there is that sudden, disheartening weight of all that spare time we find on our hands that we have not trained ourselves to know how to deal with.

This one was not great, and he was not an exception, and he was among the many that did wish to carry on anyway. He had nothing better to do with his leisure than to try writing another novel, and another one, and then another. That was the reason he habitually supplied with sardonic levity now to people who inquired if he was working on anything new: Of course, was his reply—he had nothing better to do. They thought his answer a characteristic joke. *He* knew it was true. He really had no choice. Like others with the same high calling, there was not much else he could fancy in the matter of preoccupying physical hobbies or diversions. Hunting seemed bestial, fishing was foolish—you could buy fish. Tennis, golf, skiing, sailing, though reliably time consuming, did not, like dancing, strike him as a recreation sufficiently dignified for thoughtful people. Hiking maybe, but he disliked walking and was in fear of physical discomfort. He would guess that even Ernest Hemingway, notwithstanding all his fishing and hunting, must have found the barren hours burdensome when he was not fishing and hunting and no longer writing with robust assurance, and that his decline of reputation into critical and popular disfavor was terrifying and unbearable. The singular fact about the creation of fiction is that it does turn more, not less, difficult with seasoning and accomplishment—for proof, study the concluding chapters of the biographies of famous authors—and then there is still all that cumbersome amount of spare time to spend one way or another if you do dare to stop. Minutes take hours. Hours last months. Even infidelities absorb fewer afternoons and early evenings as lust wanes away to desire, and desire to nostalgic lamentation. Especially after that inevitable move into the country, where logistical difficulties are large, and circumspect opportunities fewer. And so many of even our highest and most dedicated literary achievers come upon a leaden sadness in late life while they dwindle into inactivity and settle into the forlorn despair that proves the endgame too often.

How many naps can a reasonable person take a day—in the late morning, the early afternoon and late afternoon, before dinner, then after dinner on a couch in the living room preceding bedtime—before he fairly judges himself stagnant, moribund?

For a speech he had committed himself to give at a university in South Carolina toward the end of the current academic year, he had already started studying the biographies of well-known authors, and he was toying already with the surprising idea of titling his lecture "The Literature of Despair."

This author was determined to go on, to keep striving to go on. He often appropriated as his own personal infirmity the concluding words of the unnameable voice in Samuel Beckett's *The Unnameable*, "I must go on. I can't go on. I'll go on," although the afflicting woes were not even remotely the same. He rounded them out with a remembrance from Tennyson's "Ulysses": "To strive, to seek, to find, and not to yield."

He would go on.

But with what next, then?

A novel about a novelist was ineluctably not a consideration, already passé in a category already made too full by a swelling number of published American authors. Definitely out of the question. As were any about a disgruntled academic or younger secondary school teacher with literary aspirations who, if female, flounders into disappointing love affairs with disappointing males she soon can no longer even look up to, or if male, stumbles ridiculously into exasperating extramarital ones.

Definitely not, not by him—no, definitely not again.

Unhappy marriages, maladjusted families—what families were not? Very bad parent-child relationships seen close-up with a dissecting eye required an intensity of absorption in such subject matter he knew he could no longer muster and sustain. And anyway, women seemed much better at those now—women, in fact, seemed so much better at all sorts of things these days, including, he quipped to himself, without specifying, behaving like men. Historical figures were the terrain of his betters, who appeared to find them less and less inspiring as those efforts accrued. Mysteries, murders, melodramatic adventures were not in his range: he knew they were not his métier and not his forte. Spy stories, suspense stories too. Gangland? An action story of suspense, raw sex, and criminal violence? Mafia stuff? Maybe, maybe. Along the way in his research for a somber tome about something else he had picked up peripheral bits of information about gangsterism and killings in the early days of Coney Island, and the thought of a Coney Island mafia novel flickered in his mind, however fleetingly, each time he thought of doing a novel the motion picture industry might want—but what would it be about? That too would necessitate an elongated, convoluted amount of flashy plotting that he did not feel he had the time left to evolve and that he did not wish to think himself capable of executing with dexterity. That was one of the things he appreciated most about Borges, who detested plots, as well as such other staples of storytelling as characterization and motivation. Even the longest fictions by Borges were mercifully short. By now this one too had come to detest plots and to deplore the requirement of coping with their contrived complications. But Borges had not sold any of his works to the movies or American television, that peculiar measure of success that would have gone far to confirm him to a national audience as a writer of some stature and validate his works as sound literature. War seemed finished as a subject, at least until a new big and better one came along. Furthermore, he had already drawn one good novel from his service in World War II that had established something of a reputation for him, and he did not know what he could add to anything but his income with another. Economic injustice was common knowledge, no surprise. No outrage anymore either. Racial cruelty too. Social realism was not realistic, psychological realism was old hat. On the back burner, the back burner of his imagination, simmered the possibility of a canny sex novel. Perhaps it had been simmering too long. Innumerable others had been there sooner, sometimes more than once. And sex was old stuff too now, as commonplace in literature as in real life, even in those brassy women's service magazines. But he had secreted away in a nook of his memory and on a card in his file box an approach to a sex novel that fairly tingled with originality and impudence, a sex novel, raunchy and frank, perhaps even pornographic, but from the point of view of a woman, perhaps a housewife, but as told by, or written by, a man. On one of the index cards he usually employed for notes, he had months before lettered as a reminder, all in uppercase characters to simulate to him the title of a book itself, the words

A SEX BOOK

The eyes of people he knew, men and women, sparkled open with pleased expectation whenever he mentioned that intention in answer to the question of what he intended to work on next. That was the trick up his sleeve, his ace in the hole so to speak, he jested to himself in a punning, infirm double entendre so bad he would never offer it to anyone aloud, even when drunk. He also knew he would never write that book. A sex novel, even from the point of view of a woman, would no longer, he felt, be seemly for a man his age rejoicing in the austere ambiance surrounding his upright reputation. And even more forbidding was the sense of irre- movable uncertainty about a subject with which he no longer felt himself adequately in touch. In a cultural environment in which bunches of cheerleading teenage girls entering college boasted they were no longer virgins, had been in therapy, and were already on Prozac, he felt his civilization had bounded ahead too speedily for him to remain acquainted with all the specifics and that he had been left faltering impotently behind. No, the idea of a sex novel about a woman written by a man, though provocative and juicily promising, did not feel comfortably feasible. But what, then, could his next novel be about?

How about a novel, he joked to himself as a caprice, about a novel, with the novel itself as the narrator?

Why not?

There was spontaneous titillation in the mere idea, which was of course an impossible one. The beginning would be easy—that came straightaway to mind: "I was conceived in the brain of Dostoyevsky or Kafka or Melville. My first words were, 'I am a mean man. I am a spiteful man. I have trouble with my liver,' or, 'One morning Gregor Samsa woke up and found that overnight he had been turned into a bug,' or, 'Call me Ishmael.'"

What reader would not want to know more about what it was like to be a famous work of fiction, with the book itself as the protagonist fighting for dear life to survive?

Here was a very good and electrifying idea—but good only for a page or two, for a very short innovative piece on the humor page of some bookish magazine, with readers who would recognize the one or the other. Then what else? Where on earth could he find something different and new that neither he nor scores of others had not already written about or were not in the process of completing even while he dawdled? If not on earth, then perhaps he could find something in the heavens. Why not? There were constellations named after humans and animals with some kind of ornamented narrative history. Ursa Major, Ursa Minor, Cassiopeia,

Orion the Hunter. But then he would have to get busy doing research in astronomy and, worse, much worse, astrology. The people he'd have to find to talk to about astrology, he guessed with incipient and immediate misgivings, would likely be women, adamant beyond reason in astrological faith; it was likely they'd be vegetarians, and very generous sexually. He'd met them before and had, he recalled still one more time, been in love with two, very far back. He easily and tenderly envisioned the two young women with whom he'd had these passionate friendships long, long in the past. One, he'd been told, had since married and borne children; the other was in the newspapers occasionally as a successful figure in entertainment publicity. Both had dealt tarot cards too. He smiled when he remembered much more. With one, he had for almost a year ingested for a complete daytime meal a giant tumbler of brewer's yeast, lecithin, choline, and banana mixed in a blender with yogurt, skim milk, and honey, the whole in a concoction as vile as anything he could recollect or imagine. For almost a year. Such was the dulcet folly of unselfish love. By one of these sweethearts he'd been taught to recognize the bustle of agitation writhing beneath the sweet melodies and harmonies in the divine chamber music of Schubert. By the other, he had been introduced to the lovely formality of Tantric erotic art. For both he had gladly lost weight to appear more supple and athletic, to the world and to himself. Thinking of both, he often had the whimsical daydream of meeting with each of them at least one more time in a wistful mixing of mutual fondness and wondering what would occur. He was certain he knew what would occur: he knew, despite the disfigurements of time, he would find himself in love with both again, for a day or two or longer, for each was intelligent, humorous, and perceptive, and each would find herself again in love with him—at least for a day or two, for he was intelligent, humorous, and perceptive also. In one of his invented scripts he even envisioned a husband telephoning unexpectedly to arrange the tryst because the woman was not entirely well and had expressed the wish to see him at least once more. He had no doubt the meetings would unfold wonderfully. He was, after all, an optimist. He was, after all, a novelist.

But the stars as characters were out of the question also— today we knew too much about them for personification. They were on fire and billions of years afar. But the planets? He remembered there were seven or nine of them endlessly circling the earth, each with a name. Each name with a mythological history. And such histories. Wars, sex, violence. In the beginning was an awesome family drama of unthinkable ferocity covering three generations, from Uranus, who swallowed his children at birth lest a son displace him, until he was overthrown by one of them, Cronus, who did the job by cutting off his penis—and who then in turn buried all *his* children with the same trepidation, until he was overthrown by Zeus, who then in his turn started out by swallowing his first wife and first offspring. Such people, such gods. Desire too. Venus and Mars separated by Earth in their eternal orbits as they lusted to get back into the adulterous bed with each other. Even Earth—Ge or Gea, he would look it up—had an abundant sexual history as the first mother, mating with the heavens. And far out somewhere was Pluto, that king of the underworld, with his kidnapped bride, Persephone, who had to be allowed back on earth every six months if vegetation was to vegetate and crops were to sprout again and flourish.

An obvious wisecrack would be to guess that the god Pluto, Hades to the Greeks, looked forward with impatient relief to that annual six-month vacation from his wife. Pluto—Hades—was a problem: the planets bore Roman names, but the adventures were those of the Greek gods and mortals. He could glide by that one easily in an explanatory sentence or two, exactly as we're doing right now. Then there obtruded another badgering technicality: the planets were *not* circling the earth, endlessly or otherwise; they were circling the sun, and Earth was but another one of them, which was something the makers of these first myths did not know. But that was okay, too, because Ge or Geia or Rhea, Mother Earth, the mother of them all, figured in the early stories too, coaching Cronus to sever the genitalia of his father, and later sheltering Zeus until he was ready to overthrow *his* father. Seven or nine planets, Mercury-Hermes was also among them, all related, circling endlessly, circling helplessly, imprisoned by gravity in their inescapable orbits, what were they doing up there, what were they thinking? Seven or nine chapters and stories, maybe more?

It's a thought, we thought, the elderly author and I.

ZEUS

The gods of the Greeks were crazy too. One of them created mankind from a figure sculpted in clay. So inflamed was Zeus by this unauthorized act of initiative that he punished Prometheus first by exiling him and next by chaining him to a mountain crag with an eagle feasting on his liver all day long. Zeus saw to it that the liver restored itself each night so that the racking tribulation of Prometheus could resume in full the next morning. Prometheus committed other acts that defied and enraged Zeus: he stole fire from the gods and furnished it to man for the warmth and cooking the new, mortal breed of his needed to survive, to be fruitful and multiply, and he taught them the necessary arts and crafts. Zeus was incensed by it all. The way he felt, mankind could have frozen to death to the last human and faded from existence as idiotically as they had all been brought in. Who needed them down there, he objected, who wanted them? Anyone wishing to be a friend to humans would not have created them to begin with.

There was a cryptic curse on Zeus that endangered his own existence. Zeus knew about the curse but didn't know what it was. Prometheus knew but for a long time refused to tell. (*We* know: Zeus would be overthrown and replaced by the son of an immortal woman destined to bear a child more powerful than his father.) Prometheus would not reveal to him the identity of the goddess until Zeus released him from the mountain to which he was chained. Zeus would not release him until Prometheus told him. It was a Catch-22. Until Zeus finally did find out, he ceased copulating with immortal women on land, sea, and Mount Olympus, with the solitary exception of Hera, his faithful and steadfast wife. And along about that same time, as if by chance, Zeus started to undergo a caring change of heart toward the race of men and women Prometheus had introduced on earth, particularly when he began to notice how comely the women could turn out to be, and the males too. In time, he took a fancy to the youth Ganymede, raped him, of course, and was so enthralled with him afterward that, assuming the form of an eagle, he snatched him up in his talons and abducted him to the heavens into immortality, where he kept the beautiful young man close by ever afterward as a cupbearer to himself and the other gods.

Prometheus?

Prometheus? Find out more about Prometheus to see if he was one of the immortal sons of Zeus. If yes—oh, do we have a riveting direction to follow in the long, malignant conflict between immortal father and immortal son. If not, what can we do with this book that has not already been done by Homer, Hesiod, Aeschylus, Sophocles, and Euripides, and by Percy Bysshe Shelley and Philip Roth too?

Oh, heck. Prometheus was not the son of Zeus, but the son of one of the Titans who helped Zeus overthrow his father, Cronus, and supplant him.

But . . . Maybe . . . Maybe?

Maybe this one's even better.

HERA

My husband is my brother. Among us gods that's not so unusual. But still doesn't excuse him for the way he acts and it doesn't explain him. Every time I turn away to take care of something of my own he's off after another woman. He turns himself into a bull, an eagle, a swan, maybe even a snake, for all I know, or a shower of gold. With Alcmene he simply turned himself into the image of her husband for part of the evening. And because of that, I had another rival to hate, and his son from that one too, Heracles, Hercules to you, to try to get even with for the rest of his life. I'm a jealous god; just because I'm a chaste goddess don't believe I'm not. And I've been kept really too busy much of the time taking my revenge on all these other rivals of mine he takes a fancy to and pounces on. He spies one, rapes and impregnates her, then abandons her to bear and rear his child. What is it with these men? First they want so many of us, and once they have us, they value us so much lower. Even that so-upright Apollo of ours is seized by that same fever every once in a while and goes racing wildly and jealously after nymphs and dryads. Poor them. And Ares does it with that sluttish Aphrodite just about every time her husband looks away to get busy at his forge. There've been those rumors about Zeus and her doing it together at least one time long back. Unproven—yes. Unfounded? Who knows? Certainly, Aphrodite gambols around about me as though it could have happened. What could I do even if it's true? Not much. She is a goddess too. I couldn't transform her into a cow, as I did with Io, much as I'd like to, or a bear, as I did with Callisto, or hoodwink her into burning herself up, as I did with Semele when I teased her into begging Zeus to appear to her in all his glory. You'd think my husband, Zeus, would be much more careful once he found out there's a mystery woman somewhere destined to bear a son stronger than his father. If Zeus is ever the father it's all over for him. I have to wonder about him and all this sex, about all men, and to wonder about me. I'm not bad looking, I'm beautiful in a stately and dignified way; in fact, I'm Junoesque, if I say so myself. I do say so myself. Although when dazzled by vanity once, I let myself contend and lose out in the judgment of that Trojan prince Paris in the contest against Aphrodite and Athena to see which of us he thought the fairest. We offered bribes. I spoke into his ear and offered him greatness among all men if he chose me. But that callipygous Aphrodite wantonly displayed herself and the smooth shape of her buttocks in an immodest turn with her arms raised and her breasts up and promised him the most beautiful woman in the world for a wife if he picked her. I forget what Athena offered. Guess who won.

I've nursed a spiteful hatred for that Trojan prince Paris

and everyone in that whole city ever since. Who could blame me? And when the Greeks sailed off to make war there, I did what I could to support them, while Aphrodite, that cunt, favored Troy.

I don't think I understand men. Why does Zeus need—want—other women? I lie alone often now and try to picture things. How does Zeus feel to them? Do they really mind, knowing it's Zeus? Or are they pleased to be ravished by him? I try to put myself in Leda's place. It could be kind of thrilling, I guess, being overpowered by a huge male swan, especially after realizing it was Zeus. And Danaë? I think I might be flattered also if he ever came descending back on me in our bedroom as a shower of gold. I'd like to see him take the trouble to surprise me like that, even once. But that doesn't happen. He won't waste tricks like that on me. He never does, he knows he doesn't have to. When he comes to me it's never with anything new, it's always just the same, always just the same old god.

Even notions that dissolve into nothing have value to the professional author for the hours, days, or weeks they consume before they prove worthless and expire into metaphorical wreckage: they engage the intelligence deeply and hopefully in something he most wanted to do and, until futility reared a lethal head, most enjoyed being absorbed with. This was not, of course, the way this author permitted himself to look at what he thought of as his work and some critics occasionally chose to speak of as his art. Killing time, merely pursuing a distraction to ward off the doldrums, certainly was not the paramount motivation underlying his creative incentives when he had first started out earnestly some fifty years before, and was not, to his mind, the goading impetus now.

It was, however, the way Polly, his current wife, had silently come to regard it in this present, longest interval of uninspired and sometimes panic-stricken indecision. Certainly, he was more pleasant when engrossed and preoccupied than when idle and frustrated. Polly had learned by now never, not even in their most confidential discussions, to volunteer this opinion other than in cooperative assent after he had voiced it first, and she never did, unless, as frequently occurred, she forgot. Polly was kind and obliging in character and timorous by nature and she desired more than anything else to circumvent all unnecessary discord in this second of her two marriages. Past fifty now, and rounding out into enhancing plumpness as many of us are prone to do as we smoothly graduate into our golden years, she did not even dare speculate as to where she might be forced to go if this marriage too came to an unfortunate conclusion in divorce.

His name was Eugene Pota, because that's what I want it to be, and in ethnic background he was central European or Turk, I guess, and maybe partly or fully Jewish. But none of that enters into it. He had four adult children from the earliest two of his three marriages and they too are no more essential to this story than a sudden downpour would be or the sudden effluence of the musky fragrance of honeysuckle or magnolia, whatever. Where these others live and what they are like and do is none of our business. There were grandchildren too in unspecified, increasing numbers, who also have no part in this narrative, so they as well have been settled a distance away. Polly's two daughters from her first marriage were grown and also lived independently somewhere else. It becomes so much tidier with all of them placed elsewhere, emancipating all of us from the problems and traits in personality they would have to be given if brought around.

Pota's most recent novel—some said it was his "best written" since his first—had been published eighteen months earlier, after he had already passed the age of seventy-three. The reviews were just about unanimously respectful, which was disappointing, and the sales were slightly better than forecast, and this was disappointing also.

He had seen much better days when starting out, with novels that had kindled outbursts of cheerful applause and won for him a growing number of eager boosters who had elevated successive works of his near to the top of all national best-seller lists and had sustained them there for nearly whole seasons. That did not occur anymore. Normally, with the pleasant turmoil of publication and the gratifying travel for advertising American and foreign editions, close to a year could pass between the publication of one work and his passionate eagerness to cast himself wholly into another that had ripened in his mind as an embryonic ideal while he was still egocentrically enveloped in his satisfaction with the one just out. Now, one year and a half later, he was without a plot, at loss for a subject, and had no clear idea what to move on to next. Now, he grieved at times, he had perhaps, in a way perhaps paradoxically unlucky, lived too long and done too well: he had functioned too long, been around too long. Like others among his peers of comparative age, he had earned, and suffered, the illustrious fate he had hungered for from the start, the station of finding himself prominent, acknowledged, accepted, assimilated, and . . . familiar. Taken for granted.

After all, a new talent can be discovered only once. And astonish hardly more often than that.

Furtively, Polly studied him and brooded about him, and about herself. She cared for him more than he seemed to know, and she felt most comfortable with her own position when he was in ebullient good health and buoyant humor. She truly did not know how she could fare without him, if ever she had to. Her first husband, conceited and patronizing with a flourishing business success that had amazed them both and that neither had expected, had altered with time and an array of tempting alternative opportunities had come, with the exit of the last of the children from the household, to criticize and behold her, the woman he'd been married to a long time, as, in her words, ordinary, aging and dull. Each of these accusations stung: she took them personally, narrowly. His name's not important, nor his occupation, since he has no part in this narrative either and probably won't be mentioned again. She could not pause to see objectively that no man's wife, in Pota's pragmatic view, was not dull in comparison to the sprightlier object of his newest adulterous infatuation. About the oppressive allusion to her age, Pota could be courtly and consoling, and when they commenced their intimate friendship, he was able to compliment her truthfully with the declaration:

"You know, Polly, to me you're still a young piece of ass."

It was the nicest thing a gentleman had ever said to her, she felt at the time, and thought so still.

And indeed she was, or more accurately *had* been, for marriage and middle age had tended to moderate the lubricious zest she had at first shown so as to be entirely pleasing to him as his voluptuary. Marriage and middle age sometimes do that to women, he reflected often. It was true she was not extraordinary, and that was another virtue to him at that stage of his life. With three marriages and innumerable romantic escapades in between, and sometimes simultaneously, he'd had more than enough of vivacious, carefree women who were young, glowing, and . . . extraordinary.

She was distressed just about daily to see him restless and

dejected over his inability to immerse himself in something convincingly worthwhile. A normally convivial person of even temper, she had noted that sallies by her at jolly encouragement like "Finished the new book yet?" evoked a reaction in him sharply different from the one intended, and she never made them anymore, except when she forgot. Talkative and good natured, she commonly had very much more she wished to say than he cared to hear, and she often found herself in what she thought of as a Catch-22: she must either refrain from talking to him about things she wished to talk to somebody about, in effect surrender her right to freedom of speech, or risk his irritated, sometimes furious discontent by boring him loquaciously, and neither seemed fair. I can give you examples, more than you want, but you wouldn't like them after a while. And neither would he. Pota would not enjoy having to hear them again, and Polly would not enjoy having them written about. And this book is about him, not her; it's a tract in the form of a fiction about a life spent writing fiction, but she might not choose to see it that way.

Pota might listen to her as long as he could with a face set resolutely in glazed impassivity, as though she were not there talking to him, until she caught on. Or he might say, harshly, "So what?" or, "Why are you telling me that?" Another tactic he had sneakily devised was suddenly to bellow "WHAT?" at her almost as forcefully as he could, as soon as she began, as though she had unforgivably infringed on him while he was in deep thought with an interruption he'd been unable to hear or bear. His unexpected shout never failed to take her back with something of a fright and cause her to reconsider. Each time he heard her repent with a humble "Never mind," he felt with entertaining malice that he had scored another point in this interminable friction between them. He had learned, when she called out from another room something that was indistinct, not to request her to repeat it, and he never did, except when he forgot. Sensibly, they sought a middle ground and compromised.

And inevitably, of course, they both suffered.

Polly had lightly freckled, rounded cheeks circling and accenting her cornflower blue eyes, twinkling eyes marked by only faint traces of crow's-feet, but who cares about that? This is a book about a well-known, aging author trying to close out his career with a crowning achievement, with a laudable bang that would embellish his reputation rather than with a fainthearted whimper that would bring him only condescension and insult. We, he and I, don't have leisure or patience for a book ponderous with descriptive details of character and place, although we still had reverence for works dense with them, by Tolstoy, Proust, Joyce, to name but a few . . . and Dickens too, whose "solitary as an oyster" alone should put him in some hall of fame for similes.

Descriptive details of place and character take time, deplete energy, aren't always necessary. Worst of all, we have never been much good with them. Or much good with intricate plots propelled by swift-paced action. It's a reason we've not done so well with sales to the movies.

More than once, Polly had heard Pota quote as an apothegm from Freud that a person to be happy had to be able to love and to work. These days, both saw, Pota was not having much luck with his capability at either. It was a comfort to Polly that Pota no longer displayed the same sexual urgency, vigor, and versatility he had brandished like a standard at the beginning—she too—in their first few years, or first year, or maybe first *half* year, of their mutual and unrestrained commitment to attachment. News of the widely publicized development of a male potency pill had filled her alarmingly at first with an almost numbing dread he might immediately come springing back upon her as the maddened, wrestling satyr he had seemed at the start, overlooking her incipient chronic arthritis of the neck and hip, her chronic bursitis at the left shoulder, and forgetting that the wrenching of tendons and ligaments long unused to strain could amount to a grueling exertion with a critical impact upon the climactic enjoyment of her sexual desires and pleasure. Forgetting too that the lubricious liquors of arousal no longer flowed in either of them as copiously and responsively as at the dawn of their romance. It was of great relief to Polly that he showed no amplified interest in the new sexual aid and elected to abide contentedly in the weekly, twice-weekly, or biweekly program between them that had become something of a rather tame and unvarying, orderly ritual, one with a restricted number of likely outcomes that were always unpredictable but not unforeseen. Pota, whose envy of rivals was never covetous, was titillated to admiration by the John Updike line in *Bech at Bay* about the man past seventy who coupled with a girl in her twenties: "but they worked with that." A gem like that one, Pota considered, was more precious than rubies and also belonged in some hall of fame, not just in a book of quotations. Always now in the matter of their love life it had become his habit to busy himself in work and other things while waiting for Polly to find herself affected sentimentally and initiate the amorous activity, and then always he would immediately respond in like kind and with like purpose. To himself, he rationalized his loss of aggressive lust with the excuse that he had already been disappointed far too many times in taking the stroking initiative and proposing that she cease doing what she was doing and lie down for him right then. He had maintained to her, and still asserted to himself, that if he could not have her when he wanted her, he would simply stop desiring her passionately, and that had turned out to be true.

Almost all his adult life, he ruminated frequently, and had once, just once, said so aloud, he'd had at least two women to enjoy sex with whenever he wanted to. Married now to Polly, he often did not have even one.

They kept tactful secrets from each other: he did not mention that he had obtained a prescription for the blue pill and had hidden the sealed vial in the very rear of a drawer with his socks, where he knew she would find it when she replaced the laundry; she had found it and in turn said nothing. And then she waited to see what would ensue. And kept waiting. And then, despite herself, she'd been disappointed and for a little while had felt neglected, and rejected, because he made no move to test the remedy with her or anyone else. The seal on the vial remained unbroken. In her sulky wonderment, she in her turn had forgotten that he too suffered the discomforts of arthritis and bursitis, of stiff limbs, shortness of breath, and had knee and lower back problems to boot. That he grew older every day. And that furthermore, dressing and undressing took longer for him than ever before, and even sitting down, without crashing, was not so easy anymore either.

By and large, if the truth be told, Polly, like all of us, often *was* dull, and this was another one of her attributes that appealed to him. He was dull too and knew it, and rarely extended himself at home to be otherwise, except in the company of others, when there might be some point in seeming attractive and witty. *Ordinary, aging,* and *dull*—those were exactly the qualities he'd hoped for in a woman at the time they'd met, and the two of them now regularly attained with each other that functioning and unremarkable domestic serenity that is often identified as marital bliss. When they bickered now it was only over annoyances and small peculiarities of personality. They could not even disagree over politics. Pota, a lifelong liberal radical, hardly cared what happened in Washington anymore. His feelings about government were spare and uniform: he detested both political parties, pugnaciously despised all incumbents, and was pugnaciously antagonistic toward all challengers to displace them, and to all political attendants. Anyone seeking public office was not worthy to hold it, was an aphorism he postulated that he tried not to repeat too often. When he fantasized about leaving Polly, as he often did in brief moods of indignation, he fathomed from the first that only his irritation at the time was directing him along that track and that his hopes were an unrealistic daydream. Equally puerile was his persuasion that when he imagined *her* leaving him, he imagined himself making no protest to dissuade her. But at all times in these fictional scenarios of his there was another woman waiting in the wings who would very soon make a compensating entrance to replace her, someone delightful he had not yet met, who would be just as efficient at running the small house for him at the seashore and the small apartment in the city, and as good at cooking, sewing, and hanging pictures, mending gates and leaky faucets and other such things, and infallibly perfect for him in all other feminine respects at every moment of every day; and he well knew, when he was offstage outside the perimeter of his reverie, that there was no such person anywhere. As it stood, a woman who would make his dinner reliably and wait on line in supermarkets and specialty food stores was worth more than rubies too. Polly, the daughter of a high school principal in a far-flung school district in Nebraska, was deft with things like a hammer, wire strippers, and an electric screwdriver and saber saw.

Pota had arrived at that age, he bantered openly even in mixed company to friends, of whom they both had many, in the country near the seashore as well as in the city, where falling in love again was no longer cost effective.

To those who appeared confused, explaining what he meant was easy. Others who had lived through episodes of such type needed no explanation.

Divorce was not cost effective either.

Marriage *was* cost effective.

The thought of living separately did radiate certain charms, but only if he had someone always at hand to do the laundry, clean the house, and change the electric lightbulbs. Like a character he'd once conceived in one of his novels, he would sooner starve than attempt to cook another meal.

As regards his present difficulty with his work, there was an occasional self-justifying speculation that he was perhaps idealistically setting his sights too high, maybe impractically attempting too much. They had talked about that together in relaxed conversations over Armagnac or other after-dinner liqueurs when they were feeling close (and when they were feeling close over liquor, she could be depended on to grow affectionate and started caressing him in ways that ultimately led them to bed with corresponding desires). His was the grandiose determination that his next novel, possibly his last, should be hailed as among his best, and win for that year of publication a literary prize or two of high caliber, prizes that had eluded him thus far throughout his career, although he could not resolve yet what that novel was going to be, or be about. No collection of short pieces, and no more short pieces for magazines . . . not a purely comic novel, because comic novels didn't sell well and usually did little to solidify an intellectual reputation . . . no roman à clef: he could think of no one left in public life he wanted to write about and only a few about whom he even wanted to read . . . no fables, fantasies, or allegories, no sir, not for him. Experimental, perhaps, but no novelties or trickery, absolutely not. What he wanted was—he was not sure.

The preliminary groundwork for the lecture he had contracted to give on the very sad endings to the lives of so many famous authors had introduced to him the disheartening number of late, lesser, smaller, weaker works that had shaped in a downward curve the accomplishments at the close of their celebrated careers. In the question and answer period following that speech, he might, if it appeared discreet, easily rattle off a dozen examples. It was not easy, in fact, after Henry James, to think of exceptions. But James was a mysterious figure. Equally mysterious was the opaque, oft-quoted statement by T. S. Eliot that Henry James had a mind "so fine that no idea could violate it."

Pota had given up asking himself, and others: Just what the hell does that mean?

He had not a clue, and for his own edification he greatly preferred such down-to-earth quotations as that made by the duchess of Marlborough, in diary or letter: "Last night my Lord returned from the wars and pleasured me twice with his boots on."

There was no confusion about that one, was there? Pota made a mental note, again, to read up on the diary or letters of the duchess of Marlborough, after, he guessed, he had finished with Pepys, if he ever finally brought himself to take that one on. Pota turned his thoughts back around to the proper topic of his present melancholy meditations. To his analytical mind, it appeared that this general slackening in endeavor and scope toward the finish was indication of a failure of will rather than talent. I would not let the theory cross his mind that those authors, like he, had depleted most of the power and the creative resources of imagination. After all, he reasoned, they knew as much and more as they ever did, had a longer, wider experience with the techniques of the craft, and if the memory was not always as graciously yielding as formerly, there was always Roget's *Thesaurus* to replenish the vocabulary. As for tiring sooner, one could always labor one hour instead of two and take extra naps during the day, couldn't one?

He would not, for example, he confided once to Polly in a furtive whisper, and almost came close for an instant to believing it, have wanted to close out his career with *Felix Krull, Confidence Man* after *The Magic Mountain*, the Joseph books, and *Dr. Faustus,* and *Tonio Kröger* too, although he would have given his eyeteeth to have written it earlier.

That late novel by Thomas Mann was just about the right size for someone Pota's age to take on now. Not so short as to seem fraudulent when presented as a novel and not too massive for someone like him to undertake with the actuarial odds not too frightening against his chances of completing it. Among the first of the works to appear to him as a potential model was Camus's *The Fall*, because of its restricted length and deep philosophical seriousness, albeit, he recalled, he'd been at a loss to account for the high regard as fiction with which it was received and the broad public favor it found when first published. A second, recent reading did not enlighten him. Polly, a better, more forbearing reader than he— she had gone through such as Proust and Robert Musil without a qualm of hesitation—had not been able to connect personally with it either. The *Portrait of the Artist as a Young Man* was another the right size for him too, and with the right subject matter; but Pota, to his current regret, had already published as a memoir his autobiographical reflections on his childhood and family life in Coney Island and had interwoven segments of his war and life experiences afterward into almost all his novels. John Barth's *The Floating Opera* was another wonderful work of manageable size—obviously Pota could not at his age embark on a monumental task that might take as long as even five years! He knew he was missing that special acumen of present-day British novelists like Ian McEwan or Anita Brookner for compressing intricate fields of action and large geographical vistas into disciplined short texts of a couple of hundred pages. "Notes from Underground" and "The Metamorphosis," though both too short for a full-length tome, would have been right up his alley. He could have, would have, expanded them pliantly into acceptable size with tart dialogues and scenes glittering with symbolism and caustic cynicism, satire, and mordant psychological insight. But both had already been written. People seemed to have forgotten Faulkner's *The Bear*, and there was a thought. But let him try to imitate it and they'd sooner remember, as they were vengefully prompt to recall Faulkner's *As I Lay Dying* each time someone presumed to adopt its form or content. And what could someone like him do with anything of mythical stature like *The Bear* in a New York or East Hampton setting, and what did he know about anywhere else? And how could anyone even begin to imagine a Faulkner, or any of his unique works? Could anyone imagine the Melville of *Moby-Dick* or *The Confidence Man*? I had to recall to Pota's mind, pooling now as it was with self-pity, that Faulkner had died in a drunken fall from a horse at sixty-five and that Melville had died wretchedly in poverty, obscurity, and without a publisher for some later works that have now come to be regarded as among his best. Pota, as comfortably settled as he was ever going to be and with no dearth of publishers eager for a look at his next work, though with much reason to feel sorry for himself, was at least in those crucial respects far better off than both.

But it would be easier to rewrite *The Iliad*.

Though, by nightfall that day he was beginning to have second thoughts about *The Iliad* and Hera as a heroine and narrator; and when he awoke the next morning it was with his faith in Hera wafting away like milky zephyrs with the morning mist. Goddess or not, what would he have on his hands for subject matter but another complaining woman with a philandering husband she could do nothing about? He's already presented that one in his fiction, and more than once. Unless, by chance, it turned out she had a busy secret love life of her own! We did not even have to research that one. Hera, though one time foolishly vain and led by pride into that losing beauty contest against Aphrodite, was the goddess of marriage, protector of the hearth and the family, and she had none. She was a scold, chaste and nagging. Probably, in his hands, she would turn out to be more of a Jewish wife than a Greek one. Even with that word *cunt* he daringly had given her. Pota was not easy with it, but *cunt* was another disreputable word that, like *fuck*, was working its way up into an admissible position in the modern American vocabulary, especially among women. Girls now used it freely. Mothers used it in mild rebuke to daughters, daughters as a conversational complaint with mothers, those cunts. Soccer moms were at ease with their new mannish vocabulary, and so now was Tom Sawyer's Aunt Polly.

Pota thought of *Lolita.* Then he remembered Nabokov's *Pale Fire,* which, though an original in conception, was nevertheless a perfect work for the erudite audience Pota believed he still had. But that impish archfabricator Nabokov had already written it, damn him! *Lolita* was not at all to his taste, but maybe a sex novel was not so bad an idea after all. The chances for a sale to the movies would be better than anything else he could think of, and the extra publicity, the notoriety, would be a bold announcement to the world that Eugene Pota was still active, with a deft, questing talent.

But alas, not by him. A sex book, a subtly pornographic sex book, was, he supposed, eternally a good idea, but sadly, definitely, not a good idea for him.

Unless—it was a good idea like this one:

A SEXUAL BIOGRAPHY
OF MY WIFE

A New Novel

by

Eugene Pota

That title tickled others too.

Pota cherished the giggly warmth with which it was embraced each time he disclosed it in conversation. Dolores howled with laughter. Even Fred, her husband, still writing critically in academic publications and reviewing books there critically too, unbent a bit and chortled audibly from the rear of the car.

"With a title like that," Fred exulted on the drive to the seafood restaurant in Montauk harbor for a standard Sunday lunch in summer, "you would not even need a book." Nelsa was gleefully curious. And her husband, Jordan, glowed and grinned in silent relish at the hundreds of salacious jokes he envisioned unrolling from a bottomless cornucopia of lascivious humor. There were occasional puzzled exceptions, mainly demure women, but only for the first instant of unbelieving surprise. And Polly too, of course. Each time the subject came up, Pota was cheered by the quizzical stares that darted inevitably and almost furtively to Polly's reddening face, seeking to divine how the idea of such a book was sitting with her. Polly, as foreseen by him now whenever the subject did come up, fidgeted always in the same mute manner of embarrassed discomfort and said nothing and laughed along quietly.

"It's not about me," she might argue almost peevishly, but only when directly asked. "At least I don't think so." And adding with a strained titter: "He doesn't know enough."

"It's a novel, for Christ sakes, not a history book," Pota would insist with a jocular absence of sincerity, trying deliberately to appear unconvincing. "Don't look at Polly. After all, I've had three wives, not just her. And frankly, I don't think I'd want to write a book about any of them, or about me. I don't think that all our sexual experiences combined are worth a book. I certainly wouldn't want to spend three or four years about any one of us, or any of you either. I have to invent, you know. I don't think any real person I've ever met has been phenomenal enough for the subject of a whole novel. Do any of you think you are? Tell me. Let me know about your extraordinary sex life."

The topic certainly proved a merry one for lively table conversation, calling forth unexpected admissions surprising even to the husbands and wives of those making them in follow-up discussions to questions Pota posed devilishly in the innocent guise of objective research. He had only to touch on masturbation in a mixed group to see the women squirm as though compromised and the men perk up waggishly in buccaneering remembrance. Between Pota and Polly the badinage about this sex book had become something of a teasing practical joke. He knew how self-conscious she became each time the attention moved from him to settle upon her; he knew she felt awkward and disapproved; he had no doubt she did not at all like the idea of his doing such a book, because she never once spoke a word about it. Underlying the levity of the exchanges with others was the comical uncertainty he let exist over whether he was serious or not. Pota's reputation for humor was well earned, in his writing and in social discourse, and it was known by his friends that he could weave the most elaborate falsehoods with the most trustworthy of faces for as long as his listeners remained credulous. Friends looked searchingly at him, trying to decide if he was genuinely serious about writing this sex book, or merely dazzling them for the moment. Pota could not have enlightened them even had he wished to, for he too did not know yet whether he was serious or not.

Judging from the reactions of his small audiences, it did seem to be a sure winner. Edith and Alan asked to see the pages as soon as he'd written them. So did Ken, and Ken's wife, Marissa, who without admitting anything about herself, volunteered to poll her female childhood friends about all their earlier sex events if Pota wanted her to. Just about everyone who knew of it foresaw felicitous prospects. A bestseller of large dimensions—the kind he'd all his professional life secretly pined and pined for. But the book did have at least one big problem: it would have to be written.

Certainly, the subject matter suggested by the title *A Sexual Biography of My Wife* encircled an ocean of recognizable material to which every reader in the world of all ages and both sexes could in one way or another relate from some degree of personal experience, conjectured or actual. But Pota in truth had not yet one distinct idea who or what it was to be about. The title was all he'd been able to get. To an author who took pride in, and had received praise from textual critics for, his keen openings and endings in even his less successful volumes, it was almost horrifying to find himself unable to think of even one good sentence with which to begin.

Exasperating to him also was that the one ideal sentence that did keep popping back relentlessly into his head had already been conceived by the English novelist Julian Barnes for the starting words in his first novel, *Metroland*. The words, Pota recalled with a kind of pouting admiration, were something like these, also by a first-person male narrator: "The first time I watched my wife committing adultery was in a large movie theater at . . . ," and so forth along that course. The clarification that followed was equal to the anticipation evoked: his wife had been a movie actress playing an adulterous role in the film on view.

Could Pota be blessed with a line like that one, he felt, he would be off in a flash. He yearned for one as good, an opening sentence commensurate with the unspoken promises implied in his godsend of a book title. Each time he sat staring in unremitting futility at the words already printed by him on a sheet of paper purporting to resemble a title page, "A Sexual Biography of My Wife, a New Novel, by Eugene Pota," the line by Julian Barnes reappeared to haunt him, and he regretted each time as though in mourning that it had not been his own.

"Polly," he said at home late one afternoon after a Sunday lunch in Montauk, interrupting her at the faux antique writing table in a corner of their spacious master bedroom that served as her desk. She knew Pota had a larger respect for personal privacy than he did for God, Congress, or the U.S. Constitution and never looked at anything there except, occasionally, for the remote control to the television set. There were letters and bills of hers and other paper stuff like that, some books in a small stack she intended to read, and, beneath a glass paperweight, a growing pile of book reviews she had clipped of books she meant to read, stationery, notepads, and a spiral notebook or two that could have served as a reminder for addresses and such or even a diary. He didn't care. "Do you remember the time you once told me about, soon after we met, when you were still a virgin and growing uncomfortable about it? How you and your friend Ruth were up on Cape Cod and wound up in one room for the night with those two young guys you had met just a couple of weeks before and—"

"No," said Polly curtly. "I don't remember anything like that."

"Of course you do," Pota urged. "How could you forget? And it was your first time in Cape Cod also. You had never been there before."

"I was never there with my friend Ruth."

"Then maybe it was Donna. You told me all about it once, but—"

"I can't remember anything about that," she lied tersely. "It was too long ago."

She was determined to offer no help, Pota saw. "Okay. Have it your way. Let's try this one. In Bermuda when you were there that one time, you got drunk on piña coladas or something and found yourself making out in a room with one guy when you thought you were there with the other one—"

She cut him off again. "That never happened, not to me."

"Okay," said Pota, electing as the easier route to go along with her game. "You started to tell me one time long ago a funny story about some girl you knew and a single testicle of some guy you also knew, then the phone rang for a long conversation, and then, when I remembered, you never wanted to finish the story. What was it?"

Polly gave a scornful snort. "That must have been one of your other wives. Or one of your earlier pets or darlings, as you like to call them."

"Okay," said Pota. "You were one of them, you forget. Have it your way on that one too. Let's try this one. It's something I should know but don't. Tell me, when a woman sits down to urinate—"

"Should I fix dinner tonight, or would you rather eat out? This is starting to sound depraved."

"You decide. I know it does, but if I'm going to write anything from a woman's point of view, there are things I ought to find out."

"Find out from someone else."

"You don't remember that one either?"

"You never like to decide, do you? You always leave it to me."

"Neither do you," was the retort from Pota. "The decision I made was to leave all such decisions about dinner to you. You don't like this idea of my sex book, do you?"

"That's got nothing to do with me."

"Sure it does, if you don't want it. We live together. It embarrasses you?"

"Well, you can see what people think, can't you? And how they all look at me? They think it's going to be about me, or us."

"That's just for now, and we're all kidding around. They won't think so when they read it. A book like that by me would have to be much more about the man than the woman. I'll give it up if you want me to. Just say so. I haven't gone far."

"No, don't you dare give it up," Polly exclaimed with

some alarm and a tense titter of a laugh. "Everyone seems to think it's a good idea."

"Of course it's a good idea. But I'll stop if you want me to. I've got other good ideas. Tell me, honey. If a novel by someone else came out with that title, would you want to read it?"

"Yes. I wouldn't want to wait."

"So? Should I stop?"

"Don't stop. Just stop talking about it if you can, even as a joke. If you want to do it, go ahead and do it. It sounds too good to give up. It's not the sex book I mind. It's these questions you've now started asking me. I'm not a young pussy anymore, you know."

"There are things I should know, if I'm going to continue."

"Learn them someplace else. I just don't remember. And if I did, I wouldn't want to talk about it with you anymore."

"Fine, then. But this book will make you famous too. I'll give you sections to read as I do them to make sure there's nothing in them you mind."

"I can *hardly* wait." This time she spoke dryly, stressing sarcasm. "Try not to put too much of me in."

"You won't be there at all."

"But people will think so. Use your other wives. Or your earlier girlfriends. They might have better stories."

"Maybe. I'll let you read those also."

"I can hardly wait for those, too. Oh, Gene, don't put anything aside, for me or anyone else. Just go to work. You're so much happier when you're working, on anything, and so am I. Just try to write another good book."

"What the hell do you think I'm doing?" Pota answered with a snort, and angrily turned away across the room toward his own table, with another note for his sex book I'd just put into his mind, for a card for his file of note cards. I let him recall right then the very good time long back in intercourse with a divorced medical assistant his own age who paused in her passion to inform him, in somber, almost clinical digression, that he had an external hemorrhoid. And then I allowed him to ruminate epistemologically on still another thought for this new book of ours with still one more of the contrasts he saw between men and women as they matured: he, Pota, was no longer the least bit interested, jealous, or cared about any of Polly's previous sexual escapades, in marriage or before, while her resentful enmity toward the women in his past grew more virulent with the years. And I thought I'd let him get smugly away with a simplification as to the cause: the women in his past were young at the time, and Polly saw them still that way, while Polly no longer was. I did not let him recognize right away that his sense of impertinent affront at the marital disagreement just finished was not sufficient reason to begin brooding again about the desirability of a divorce, but instead, let him brood awhile anyway, about her resistance and about the clothes closets, over which he was suddenly fuming too. Like both his previous wives, Polly, having filled her own allotted closets, which of course were always the larger ones, was now silently encroaching into his, and he found this intermittently infuriating, when he had the leisure to feel infuriated—that is, to nourish that savory petulance we all enjoy of feeling infuriated *and* self-righteous.

Pota could easily have named a few dozen more things she did that irritated him. Occasionally, he might wonder what faults Polly found with him. He could guess a few: he wouldn't go to the movies or allow her to tell him about them after she had gone without him; he was boring; he wouldn't fold his sweaters neatly when replacing them on the shelf; he did not, as she did, brush his teeth after every meal; he would not let her talk to him about things she felt she just had to talk about with someone; he flirted always, even with the pubescent daughters of neighbors and friends; women liked him—he could converse with them charmingly. He had conversed with her charmingly at the beginning, but now that they were together, like Zeus with Hera, he no longer had to. She'd adjusted to that; he would often cut her off when she tried to explain things he already understood; he sometimes found her boring and did not try to hide it; he tired much too quickly of the company of even the people he most enjoyed being with. She sensed, though she did not formulate it into these words, he was a person who, though kind, was self-absorbed and could not dedicate himself devotedly to anyone. Pota did not see himself this way at all and would scoff at the thought that he would never let himself care for anyone in the world as much as he cared for his work, and himself. Of course, I could tell you very much more about Polly if I wanted to. I could make her anything I chose, wise and capable, noisy and narrow-minded, introverted and opinionated, short or tall, blonde or brunette, benign and outgoing or malevolent and outspoken, wrapped up harshly in the discontentment of thwarted hopes or liberally addicted to lost minority causes, anything I want, really, true to life or, in one way or another, even more true than life, which is what we usually do in our fictions. But I don't want to. Of course, once having her at ease with Proust and Musil, I couldn't very well make her frivolous and uncultivated. But I could easily change Proust and Musil to *People* magazine and *Vanity Fair*, and give her an enduring taste for rock and roll music instead of having her fondly attached to the astonishing abundance of great string and piano compositions by Schubert in the last year of his life, after Schubert learned he had syphilis and presumed correctly, poor young man, that he would soon be dead. But I don't want to do that anymore, go thoroughly into character. So neither did Pota. I could develop her easily, but it's much too hard. It's painstaking and time consuming, and Pota was short of patience. The generation of writers after him, and the generation of newer novelists and short story writers following that one, are better at it now and have the gusto and the time. Let them do it. They can have it.

Polly likes Schubert because I want her to. It may seem contradictory that a woman devoted to Schubert and confidently relaxed with difficult novels should also occasionally be something of a chatterbox at home, but people are not always of a consistent piece in actuality, although they mostly seem to be in novels, except in the novels of Dostoyevsky, where all of the characters are at least half crazy, which makes them more true to the people we know, and the people we are. And Dostoyevsky is half crazy too, like the rest of us. There is a difference between Dostoyevsky and Henry James, and people have noticed that. And compensating for the offense given him by Polly's hostile appropriation of the closets (Pota soon interceded with himself) was the seductive consolation of having beneath his cupped hand in bed beside him at the start of each night's sleep the rounded hip of a woman, a woman he knew well and did not feel he had to make love to unless his hormones inclined him to want to. In the dresser drawer with his socks he had concealed the unopened vial of Viagra he knew she was certain to find. He did not want Polly to feel he needed such assistance yet. In a different place he knew she would not find, he had hidden away a second vial with an unbroken seal on the unlikely chance he might yet allow himself to fall in love again with some young woman who would eagerly have him, a young woman, say, of forty-five or fifty. Nearby, on the same second-floor level as their master bedroom, was another bedroom laid out with pillows in pillow slips and a quilt neatly folded on a spare bed for the use of whichever one of them chose to escape if the snoring or other snuffling noises of late-life respiration by the other proved disturbingly unwelcome.

Even Paul, Pota's favorite editor, responded with an untypical guffaw when Pota, with solemn mien, first made known the title of his new book to him. And Paul did not laugh easily.

"Are you serious?"

Paul always turned solemn in the presence of a book or idea he thought much of. Having worked as a conscientious editor all his life, he had suffered too many disappointments not to feel always in dread from the start in anticipation of the jumbled conglomeration of pitfalls that might lie ahead.

"Yes, I am, I think I am," said Eugene Pota. "Fred Karl loves the idea too. He said we wouldn't even have to print any pages."

"Of course not," said Paul. "Maybe we could just publish the book jacket and issue the novel with blank pages. Couldn't we do that?"

"Too bad there isn't a best-seller list for book jackets, isn't it?"

"How does Polly feel about it?"

"Guess," said Pota. "But she also agrees it might be a sure thing for a novel, and she never interferes."

"Tell me," asked Paul. "If you want to now. What's the plot, the main story? How does it go?"

"That," said Pota, "is just the problem." And now Pota was chuckling. "I guess I'll have to put in some work on that part, won't I? I've no idea yet. What would Flaubert do if he had a title like that one? Can you imagine *Madame Bovary* from the point of view of the husband? Do you think we really have to have anything printed inside between the book covers? Paul, couldn't we just have blank pages?"

"Sure," said Paul. "Or," he added, with a broad smile, "we can cut production costs and just publish the book jacket. We can forget the pages."

"Would it sell?"

"It would sell, I think. At the beginning. But not for twenty-five dollars. Maybe for ten cents. Then word of mouth would kill us. What would be your author's royalty on a book jacket price of ten cents?"

"Then I will have to think of something to write, won't I?"

"Start thinking of something."

"It shouldn't be hard. There's so much sex around."

"Something good," said Paul, who no longer was treating the thought as a practical one requiring immediate decision. "Are you truly serious about writing that particular sex book?"

"No, of course not," admitted Pota. "But let's not tell anyone yet."

"So? And meanwhile?"

"Meanwhile?"

Meanwhile, I next put into Pota's head a dynamic, resonating, taunting opening sentence for something different I knew he'd pounce upon and then would not know what to do with:

"The kid, they say, was born in a manger, but frankly I have my doubts."

Pota as predicted soon had his doubts too and resumed thinking about Hera again, and the humorous character he had started to give her, the handsome homemaker goddess in a female rivalry with the saucy Aphrodite, her husband the randy Zeus, the big cheese on Mount Olympus—there might be more opportunity in that one, after all. And then, as he was already thinking about gods and goddesses, I had him turn aside, unfruitfully as it proved, in a wasteful digression of several weeks, to:

GOD'S WIFE

God's wife had been opposed to the idea from the start.

"What do you need it for?"

"I don't have enough to do."

"What have you been doing all this time till now?"

"You know what I've been doing," said God. "Nothing."

"Why can't you keep doing that?"

"Nothing? I get bored."

"Why look for trouble?"

The true source of her misgivings was her fear of receiving from him even less attention than she'd been getting for an eternity, which was almost none; that with a new world to play with, he would not devote to her as much time as in the past, when he had nothing else to occupy him.

"What will you make them look like?"

"Like us."

"Both of us? Must you? I've been putting on weight. Haven't you noticed?"

"But smaller."

"I would hope so."

"I'll start with only one—no, two. It's not right for man to be alone, is it? Man and woman I'll make them, like us, in our own image."

"Naked too?"

"What's wrong with naked? Except when it's cold."

"What's cold?"

"It's an idea I just had. It's one of the things I want to fool around a bit with and want to find out. I'll have hot and I'll have cold. How's that sound?"

"I don't understand that. And what am I supposed to do with myself when you're busy fooling around a bit with things like cold and hot and finding out?"

"Whatever you want to. What have you been doing all along?"

"Nothing. Have you never noticed that, either?"

"Then that's what you can keep doing with yourself for the rest of eternity, if you want to. I'm getting curious about things. I want to see what happens."

"You think you know everything, don't you?"

"I do know everything. You know that."

"Then why do you have to see what happens? I think you'll be sorry."

"Why will I be sorry? And how can I know I know everything unless I try to find out? They're going to love us both, all of them. And then I'll let them be fruitful and multiply."

"I think they'll hate you. How will you do it?"

"I've been giving that some thought. I guess I'll do it with a big bang of some kind that will divide the firmament and separate the earth from the heavens and the land from the waters and all the rest of that stuff. I'll put twinkling stars up there, just for you."

"I think you're asking for trouble."

"Can't I handle trouble?"

"How do you know? Have you ever had any?"

"I know everything, don't I? They'll do what I want. I can always drown them if I get tired of it."

"And if it doesn't work out?"

"I just told you. I'll get rid of them all with a flood or another big bang. Look, I think we'll have some fun."

"What's fun?"

"I'm not sure yet. But we'll both find out."

Oh, yeah, yeah, sure, said Pota, with a scowl and an acidulous smile, leaning back from his pages in a gesture of repudiation while talking out loud to himself, again without recognizing he was doing so.

Once he got going on jokes of that ilk, he thought, he would never be able to finish, and then uneasily perceived the parallels in his *God's Wife* with the Mark Twain fragments for his "Eve's Diary," which Twain had never been able to finish either. Pota could now guess why. His spirits lifted for a moment and he smiled broadly in appreciation of Twain's entry by Eve in her diary of Adam's great scientific discovery that water flows downhill.

And of course, Pota also saw, given the beginning he was designing, he would have to start right in with a responsible new approach to the story of Adam and Eve. He would hardly have a choice.

The weakness he saw—a weakness—in his new novel *God's Wife*—and Pota was even quicker to find faults with his own work than in the novels of his friends and other contemporaries—was that the fundamental joke of the book was told with that first sentence and was over. And it was not that good a joke. Others that followed would be extended repetitions, with spoofing foolery of some best-known biblical tales that had already been done innumerable times by others in song and book and stage and cinema. If he was to continue with what still seemed to him a profuse idea, he would have to top his forerunners and add something brilliantly new that would enlarge whatever framework he chose and be intellectually and dramatically viable.

What he found to add came to him with a rush of tremendous potential, and he implanted his innovation as a timely twist in a minor reworking of lines he had already handwritten on his lined yellow pad. Not only was it good! It would, he gloried in convinced expectation, delight the feminist editors now in authority at many book publishing houses.

"I'll tell you what," said God to God's wife, wrote Pota in continuation. "You can be in charge of the women. I'm probably going to need some help keeping an eye on them all if they turn fruitful and multiply, which is what I have in mind. We'll make it a game. Okay? You against me. You've got the women, I've got the men. We'll see who's better. Let's go."

Not until the day after he polished this prose into what he hoped would be this lasting finish did it all begin to pall on Pota.

When first possessed by his new inspiration, he'd crowed lustily to Polly that he was at last back in form, and he had exuberantly flaunted his conviction that he was finally master of a new, wonderful concept.

They made love that day in the late afternoon.

She made dinner.

She hummed happily a great deal, refreshingly relieved for

him that he was working on something special again, and for herself because he had thrown away his sex book and spared her all the further chagrins of comparison and speculation that derived from his talk of a sexual biography of his wife. Not all, as it would happen, for when asked several times in the two weeks that followed, he still liked to shenanigan around with the idea of a sexual biography of his wife rather than disclose his excellent opening line for his excellent subject of God's wife and the unique tribulations inherent in that marriage to her unique husband. And Pota in his turn was relieved to at last have a wife who would not bitterly see herself mirrored and satirized in the character of every imperfect woman he portrayed in his fiction, this time not in Eve, Sarah, Delilah, Rebecca, Ruth, Jezebel, Catherine the Great, Madame Pompadour, Salome, or the Woman Taken in Adultery. One evening in that euphoric period, while he sipped Armagnac and she sipped Cointreau, they quietly enjoyed an old movie on TV they had not viewed on TV before. They succeeded in spending entire nights together in the same bed, much of it in touch with each other.

In that morning, though, after having written and rewritten his brief introductory chapter the day before, he felt stale, found himself feeling tricked in some perverse fashion by something acridly cosmic. Instead of coming awake as expected with a mind swarming with flippant twists of dialogue or apt adjectives to enrich what he had already put on paper, he saw before him a forbidding prospect that was bleak, barren, flat. He was sluggish getting out of bed. What he'd gone to sleep believing was ideal for his next major novel was revealed to him now as only a vapid anthology of formularized biblical tales unfolding in an undeviating sequence of trite stories of triumphing women very much like those in most highly successful television situation comedies. Oh, shit, he thought or mumbled aloud. God's wife would have to win almost all the time or there would be no surprise, and then, where was the surprise? And God? In a match between the sexes, God would emerge as a bungling simpleton of a husband, and that wasn't God. And if that wasn't God, then she wasn't God's wife. For a while he did not know where he was. And where was the strife between them? Hera, at least, could run away from Zeus and go into hiding, as she in fact did do once in a paroxysm of jealous pique. But where could God's wife go?

Pota was thinking sensibly, of course. It would be as tepid as if I were to try to write a book about him and Polly in which no transforming disagreements or sensational peril evolved to menace either one of them. No clash, no crisis, no climax, no resolution. No movie sale. No publisher? Not likely to occur. But that would go against the grain of everything Pota had been taught by experience and early classroom lessons, and everything he himself had taught as a distinguished professor of creative writing for the four years he'd needed to finish his second novel.

All you would get if I were to write with such undeviating tranquillity about Pota and Polly would be an even and even-tempered portrait of the artist, Pota, as an old man, and who would want to read much of that? *The Confessions of Zeno* had never been made into a blockbuster movie, and Svevo's sequel, *The Further Confessions of Zeno,* had not been a world shaker either. And after all, what more can happen to a man moving up in age past seventy-five? Illness, accident, bewilderedly hammered about disastrously again in another costly, time-consuming divorce?—or like Dickens, Ibsen, Strindberg, and maybe scores of well-known others, falling through deadening seizures of hermetic loneliness into pathetic love with an unsuitably young girl, a neighbor's child, perhaps, with a craving need for some sensitive understanding she did not feel obtainable at home, or the daughter of friends. Pota feared scandal more than anomie. What else could happen to him that was worth writing about? With Polly it might be different, an attractive woman of wide abilities and all that, but we don't care that much about her in this novel, do we? Give Pota a cancer or end his marriage and this novel about writing a novel is over and done with, and so is he.

Given the premise of the creation of the world of men and women by God and God's wife, it would indeed be mandatory to begin with Adam and Eve in the garden of Eden. That one he could handle. He was inventive enough to supply a brand-new trick or two for that setting, one that masses of others had already treated with frivolity before. But already, the joking originality he knew he could come up with also seemed stale, even before he knew what it was.

In his studio after his usual safe breakfast of cereal with fruit and strong coffee, Pota felt immobilized and cringed from his planning and his scribbling of almost two full seven-day weeks with something like an aversion of betrayed disgust, disgust with himself for a naive excess of zeal that had blinded him to the superficial mediocrity of the plots he had been contemplating so uncritically.

Oh, shit, thought Polly with sinking heart, when she saw him emerge disconsolately from his studio after less than half an hour and drift down the driveway for another walk to the beach. Pota knew now that it was a futile endeavor on which he had expended so much effort, and berating himself rigorously for his unsound judgment, resolved to put it completely out of mind, to give not one more moment's thought to these simpleminded notions by which he had been so ingenuously beguiled.

Further Notes for GOD'S WIFE

Biblical Women:
1. Eve
2. Noah's wife
3. Lot's daughters
4. Abraham's wife—Sarah
5. Isaac's wife—Rebecca
6. Jacob's wives—Leah, Rachel
7. Tamar (the first one. The one that outsmarted Judah and tricked him into knocking her up)
8. Delilah
9. Naomi—Ruth
10. Jezebel
11. Salome
12. The Woman Taken in Adultery

Mythological:
1. Menelaus's wife—Helen
2. Agamemnon's wife—Clytemnestra
3. Jason's wife—Medea
4. Electra
5. Pandora (and her box)

Greek and Roman:
1. Socrates' wife
2. Caesar's wife (?)
3. Cleopatra (?) (Some wife! Didn't she murder her brother, who was also, like Zeus with Hera, her husband?)

4. Philip's wife—Olympias (Alexander's mother, who insisted to King Philip she'd had sexual intercourse with a snake, who was really Zeus in disguise and the true father of Alexander the Great, who was therefore of divine origin. Another real cutie!)

Other Historical:

1. Duke of Marlborough's wife (?)—Sarah Churchill
2. De Sade's wife (?)
3. Freud's wife (?)
4. Freud's wife's sister (?)
5. Catherine the Great
6. Madame Pompadour
7. Margaret Thatcher
8. Monica Lewinsky (?)

GOD'S WIFE—Chapters: Notes

1. (Adam. Opening)   "Adam could not be sure Eve was not telling the truth when she insisted he had never mentioned the apple to her."

He was pretty sure she was not yet around when he had been warned about the sacred tree and the forbidden fruit. Had he told her? He could not ask the serpent, who could not be trusted, probably, and could no longer speak. Did the snake know also about the forbidden apple? Was he there at the time God warned of it? Did he know it was forbidden?

A thought: only Adam knew, and all but Adam, even the snake, were innocent.

2. (Sarah—advises Rebecca when she's been brought from her home to marry Isaac)   Sarah advises Rebecca that men are not too smart when it comes to important things and that Rebecca will have to make the important decisions for Isaac, just as Sarah has had to do with Abraham. It was Sarah who advised Abraham to have a child by the servant girl Hagar when Sarah was still barren, and Sarah who told him to expel Hagar and Ishmael after Isaac was born, so that Isaac would continue the line.

"Isaac is likable, you'll find," counseled his mother, "but not too smart. Do you follow me?"

"What," asked Rebecca, "happened to his thing?"

Sarah jumped. "Doesn't it work?" she cried, in great fright that the line of Abraham might come to an end right there.

"Oh, yes. It works a lot. But it looks so funny. Part of it's missing."

"Oh, that's his circumcision. One day Abraham walked back in and all of a sudden says that everyone there, every male, has to be circumcised. Just like that. It's like I'm telling you about men. They're good at fighting and working hard, but up here?" She tapped her forefinger to the side of her head. "It's up to us. You know what happened with Isaac and him when he took Isaac up to the mountain to sacrifice him. You don't?"

Rebecca doesn't know. She'd been brought there from far away to marry Isaac, and the news hasn't traveled.

"No? It's a tender story and almost broke my heart. Let me tell you what happened. They call it a miracle. I call it a tragedy. And I still have to wonder what the world is going to come to."

Pota paused, vigilant, as a new idea came frothing into mind and went bubbling all about his head in a germinating effervescence.

(UNTITLED: ISAAC) (?)

A New Novel

by

Eugene Pota

(Partial)

CHAPTER 1. ISAAC

"Where is the lamb?" they told me I said.

"Don't worry," said my father. "God will provide one."

I sensed something was wrong. The two servants and the ass waited down at the foot of the hill and we started up alone. I carried the wood for the fire, he brought the firestone and the knife, he carried a coil of rope. We piled up stones for the altar. He talked little, told me how to help. Then he said:

"Stand still while I tie you up."

I did not resist. I even made moves to assist when he bound me and set me on top of the wood on the altar he had let me help build. When he took up the knife to kill me I was sure it was over. When he cut me free, I wanted to cry.

We did not say much going down. My legs were shaky, my teeth chattered. I did not trust myself to speak until we were approaching the bottom and I saw the two young servants awaiting our return. I wondered later what he would have reported had he come down without me.

"I was not sure you were going to stop," I said when the path grew wider and I could draw alongside.

"The angel made me," he replied. He gave a quick smile to himself. He did not look at me. "The angel ordered me to stop. Didn't you hear?"

"I didn't hear anything. When you lifted the knife I think I was screaming."

"Then I heard the noise and saw the ram in the thicket," he went on, as though I had not said anything, and again he made that same small smile. "You heard that?"

"I couldn't hear anything. Father, please tell me this now. Did you know that the ram was going to be there? When we started out together and you took me with you, to slay me as a burnt offering?"

"I was told to do that. It wasn't my idea. God told me to do that."

"But did you know that the ram would be there? And that you wouldn't have to kill me?"

"Of course not. I would not have gone if I knew that. We don't fool around, God or me. What kind of test would it be if I knew that in advance?"

"Test?"

"Yes. I was tested. And I passed. Let me think about it now."

I did not want to look at him. I wanted never to have to look at him or speak to him again. I had to wonder what my mother, Sarah, would say when she found out.

And there it was afresh, Pota slowly began to realize, a variant on that same primal theme in Zeus and his progenitors of fathers setting out to eradicate their sons. Zeus too began that way. Like Laius and Oedipus, Pota remembered immediately. And there were Agamemnon and Iphigenia, if you wanted to include daughters. Mothers were better than fathers that way, it seemed. Didn't Ge or Gea or Rhea—he was going to have to look that up sooner or later when he had time, if it still mattered—didn't she plot with the sons to spare them death from the father? But what *would* Sarah say when she found out? That woman would not have remained silent. What woman would have?

<u>Chapters</u>: Notes

1. Sarah, narrating—She is horrified when she hears of it, is furious with Abraham, and unable to see it as he does.

2. Abraham, narrating—His staunch belief that it is God who talks to him in dreams or when the deep slumber comes over him.

3. Rebecca, narrating, all narrate in the first person—Rebecca is sent for from Haran to marry Isaac. To Isaac, when she finally is with him the first time—do not forget to put in: "My God, what happened to you?" Rebecca had come from far away and had never seen a circumcised male member before.

4. Jacob—Esau. "Put yourself in my place"—about taking Esau's place to receive the blessing from his blind father. "When I did, Esau wanted to kill me, and I had to run away. And that's how I met Rachel."

5. Rachel—Leah. "In the dark they are all the same." Leah takes her sister's place in the wedding bed, and Jacob, made drunk, doesn't discover the switch until morning.

6. Esau. "Believe it or not." "Believe it or not, I looked forward to seeing Jacob again and embracing him as my brother, and he was afraid I was still angry enough to kill him."

7. Isaac. Still living when Jacob returns, and they talk, heart to heart about . . . what? The lifelong effect of the intended sacrifice upon Isaac? Sure. And then . . . what? Or onward into Egypt with Joseph again. And then what?

Eugene Pota had not yet made his mind up which way to go with either of his two new narrative ideas. So, he decided instead to go into the city to confer about them with his two closest confidants in the publishing world, the two in whose judgment he trusted most.

Pota had smaller fear now of book reviewers and the reading public than he did of his literary agent and his favorite of two editors, and submitting *God's Wife* to one and *(Untitled) Isaac* to the other, he shrank from then presenting each of these two new ideas of works in progress to the second person after the first had responded successively and individually with what he could only regard as disappointing, and offending, coolness. Returning home from the city by bus that same day, he truly did, on the three-hour journey and for a day or so afterward, hate them both with a wounded rancor.

"It's a cute idea, Gene," said Paul over lunch, tossing back the few pages of *God's Wife*, "and if it came to me from a new writer, especially a young one, I would certainly be encouraging and interested. But is this something you really want to do?"

"I'm questioning it," answered Pota, affecting a phlegmatic objectivity to conceal his disintegrating hopes. "It's why I asked you to look at the idea and give me your opinion."

"And haven't you already done this before?"

"When?" Pota demanded sharply, his pose of neutrality shaken. "What are you talking about?"

"In your book about King David, that excellent novel," said Paul, in a tone intended to mollify him.

"They're not nearly the same, Paul. That one was an internalized family drama. This one is more like contemporary satire. And humorous, all the way through."

"But they're both from the Bible, and in a modern idiom, contemporary as you call it."

"Would you have said that to Dickens, that he'd done a book like one of his before? Or Dostoyevsky, or Balzac, that they'd already done before a book something like the new one? Or even John Grisham or Tom Clancy?"

"There's a difference, more than one."

"I know. I'm not Balzac or Dostoyevsky."

"And you're not Grisham or Clancy. And they don't come to an editor with bare ideas to see what he thinks. They bring in a book, take it or leave it, and if it's ever leave it, they then can go to somebody else. Come to me with the finished book, if you'd like. And of course I'll publish it, whether I love it or not. And if I don't want to, someone else will, certainly. God's wife is not a bad idea. I'm only asking you about this one the same thing I did about your idea for a sex book. Are you sure it's what you want to do?"

"No. That's why I'm sounding you out."

"In fact, why do anything right away if you're in doubt? Or ever? Is it money?"

"No, not right now. Not yet. That's another motivation I've lost."

"Have Erica find you some movie work if you want to keep busy."

"I've grown too old. Those kids out there don't hire people my age for scripts."

"Then why not wait until you do catch fire with some idea that's serious, sensible, and sound? You don't have to rush into anything, ever again. You've done your work. You've made your reputation. What does Erica think?"

"I haven't talked to her about this one. And I'm not going to, now that I've heard from you. It's your opinion I wanted."

"Why not take your time and wait?"

"Why not wait?" Pota echoed him. "Because I've got nothing else to do, that's why. I'm bored."

Paul snorted. "You sound like the God in that chapter you've got there. *He's* pretty amusing, at least to begin with. He's got nothing to do, so he creates the world. Why else would he make us? What happened to that sex book you spoke to me about awhile ago?"

"You made me give it up."

"*I* did? I merely asked you what goes into it."

"And that was enough."

"It might not be a bad idea. You saw what Nabokov did with *Lolita*. I also very much liked those paragraphs you sent me of Hera as a jealous wife and Aphrodite as a naughty flirt." Paul laughed quickly. "I liked it a lot when you have Hera call her a cunt. That was a funny surprise and most contemporary too."

"You never said you thought anything of it. So I filed them away. Should I rewrite *Lolita?*"

"No. And don't rewrite *The Iliad*, either."

"That's been done before too, I suppose."

"You've got nothing to do and you're bored?" echoed Paul. "Why don't you just take up golf, or bridge?"

"Why don't you just go fuck yourself?"

They parted on the best of terms.

And Erica, his astute and candid literary agent and good friend, had been no more enthusiastic about his outlined plan and first chapters for the novel about the sacrifice of Isaac.

"It's old stuff, isn't it?" she said, speaking very carefully. "I don't see why you'd want to deal with it again."

"The sacrifice of Isaac? From the point of view of Isaac? I don't know if that's ever been done before. Do you?"

"It's an old story," Erica countered, with a shrug. "And people are always doing novels about the Bible. Didn't you do one once?"

"That was King David." Pota caught himself feeling sheepish. "And that was a best-seller, remember? These are different people."

"And another thing. There doesn't seem to be that much about Isaac in the chapters you've outlined that follow. Is there? And here's another thing you might not like. If you plan to develop the book with first-person accounts in chapters by the different characters, you've already got me thinking about William Faulkner's *As I Lay Dying*."

"I know, I know," conceded Pota, surrendering. "I've already thought of that objection too. He doesn't own the copyright on structural plans, does he?"

"And your Isaac is soon out of the picture, and we're left with Jacob and probably Joseph back in the well. And then with the famine and the pharaoh in Egypt. You know, I very much liked that page you faxed me awhile ago with that jealous goddess Hera feuding with Aphrodite. That could be a funny one."

"That's old too, isn't it?"

"But different. Look, Eugene, I can probably get you a

contract for this book in a day or two, if that's what you want me to do. It won't be for a huge amount of money at this point, but you know that. You've got your following and someone will want to publish it. Half your readers may like it, half may be disappointed and fall into the category of 'Okay, but not as good as his others.' That's what happens to all of us now, anyway, doesn't it? I'm being straight with you. I thought you came to me with these pages because you wanted the truth from me."

"I do want the truth," said Pota with a sigh and a feeble smile, getting ready to leave her office. "But as always, and as everyone else, I'd like the truth I get from you to be the truth I want to hear. Thanks, anyway. We'll talk."

"What does Paul think about it?"

"I haven't shown this one to him. And I'm not going to now that I've heard from you. Your opinion is good enough."

"Thanks. We'll keep in touch."

They also parted friends, although his heart was filled with a galling sense of injury and of enmity toward her also.

Who the hell did they always think they were?

"Well, how did it go?" asked Polly finally when he was back home, and partway through the excellent dinner she'd prepared for him—black bean soup he liked from a restaurant nearby and sautéed local bay scallops—after waiting a creditably long time for him to speak about his day.

"Great," answered Pota jovially, brightening up as though with a bracing jolt of memory and good humor. "It couldn't have been better."

"Really?"

"They loved them. The two of them loved them both."

"Really?" Polly repeated incredulously, as though shed-

ding a burden of apprehension, and broke into a lustrous smile, laughing happily with plump cheeks flushing joyously as she went on. "Both of them?"

"Both of them. Both people, both books. They both loved them both."

"Then you should be very happy."

"I am."

"Then why the silence?"

"Because, darling, I've now got to write the rest of one or the other, and that's never easy."

"But that's good too, isn't it?"

"And I don't know which one to choose."

"Do both, Gene. Get to work. I'll clean up in here. I think it's wonderful."

It was refreshing to see her so pleased for him.

Polly was wearing a simple, sheer housedress with a low scoop to the bodice that drew his eyes to the twin promises implied by the swelling shapes of her full breasts. She would not be wearing panty hose, he knew. As he sat facing her across the table, a sudden desire gripped him to stand up and move to her, coax her to her feet, and put one hand down inside the neckline of her dress and his other around in back of her to squeeze her ass. Had she been a different woman or a woman still new to him, he would have acted on the impulse and lunged toward her in an instant. Now, however, he considered he was much more comfortable remaining right where he was in his chair, resting. He could wait. He gratefully appreciated the additional pounds Polly had been putting on, pounds which she for her part deplored; there was that much more comfortable feminine flesh to lie against at night and caress and embrace when he wanted to, although, he amused himself with the thought, that culminating exploit of penetration was increasingly and proportionally so much more complicated for both of them, requiring more cooperation from each than anyone had a right to expect, and often humorously conversational.

The meal over, their paths crossed in the kitchen as he was starting away to his studio to sort through his mail again and debate what work to start on next and she was beginning to clear the table. He intercepted her and took her to him in a loving hug, putting one hand on her breast and sliding his other around her for a squeeze on her backside. She submitted patiently without protest, her eyes looking past him over his shoulder, her mind obviously on some other thing somewhere else. Amused secretly, Pota wondered once again, as he released her and withdrew, which one of the two of them was farther along the road into sexual impotence. Had he been a different man, or a man still new to her, he speculated, she in her turn might instantly have dispatched whatever humdrum idea dallied in her thoughts and molded herself to him with a melting tumescence, as always had happened at their exciting, now almost unbelievable, beginning.

Funny, it occurred to him, but all the women he'd known had seemed to tire of sex before he did, but that—as far as he knew—was true of only the women who'd had sex with him. He would have to talk about that with other men.

Ah, maybe, he mused thoughtfully . . . Yes, maybe . . .

Here was food for thought, he thought.

In his study, he proceeded on both his new books by discarding the pages of each into separate folders and then drew out a third file he'd already opened, on which he intently began to concentrate.

A SEXUAL BIOGRAPHY
OF MY WIFE

A Great New Novel

by

Eugene Pota

"The first time I watched my wife committing adultery was in the movie theater in East Hampton when I . . . "

Come up with something better, damn it. Or at least as good.

Günter Grass: "Naked women, when they think they are not being observed, is not a sight you want to see." (The dwarf in *The Tin Drum* when his mother takes him to a bathing beach for nude women in Germany.)

Kurt Vonnegut: "A beautiful woman has trouble living up to her looks for very long." (Somewhere in *Timequake*, I think.)

Eugene Pota: "Women look better when they're dressed than when they are nude." (In party conversation, when only his wife, the one before this one, took exception to his remark and needed an extra minute to see it and agree. "How about lingerie? You love us in lingerie, don't you? Even in ads." "Of course," he had answered. "But that's not naked, is it?")

Duchess of Marlborough: "Last night my Lord returned from the wars and pleasured me twice with his boots on." (In her diary, or maybe her letters. Look it up.)

I'd like, gloated Eugene Pota, and perhaps even uttered the words aloud, to see those two tell me a book like this one has ever been done by me before, or by anyone else!

His passion spent, he was immediately exhausted and low in spirit again. To Polly, in another falsehood, he pleaded fatigue from the bus ride and, as happened between them only occasionally, was in bed for the night before she was.

His sleep was fitful, his morale frayed. In morbid despair, he remembered his conversations in the city that day and questioned his future. He dreaded long chapters. He felt insignificantly small, ashamed, debased. Dozing off, he had another thought, and this thought was still in his mind when he awoke.

Someone must have been telling grave lies about him, for one morning, without having done anything wrong, Gregg Sanders (Pota wrote) awoke from an uneasy sleep to find himself transformed into a sizable brown bug carting around something of a humpbacked hard shell on top of him, and with no loss of time and with a broom of stiff straw, he was ruthlessly battered out of his house into the street by his revolted family.

"Just look what he's doing this time," his enraged father roared loudly enough for the whole world to hear. He was disgusting, Gregg heard his ogre of a parent rage away, as though furiously determined to brook no contradiction from either of the two trembling women egging him on. They, his mother and his sister, stood crouching in each other's arms in a shadowed corner of the large square foyer, white faced and appalled. "I won't have him in my house that way," the bullying autocrat went on. "He was bad enough before. I'd rather have roaches again. Even a mouse. If he tries to come back in here that way, I'll step on him, I'll kill him. I'll stamp him to death. I want you to kill him too if you see him sneaking back in like that when I'm not looking. You hear? Spray him."

"Can I take his room?" his sister pleaded. "I'd like to have it as an office. I want to write a book, if I can, and try to get it published."

His father grunted as he nodded. His father, naturally, was the one wielding the broom, flourishing at the same time a folded newspaper like a deadly bludgeon should Gregg attempt to scoot back in around him.

Gregg's family unit, when not beset by an emergency of such curious kind as they were challenged by that day, was normally a typically tense, joyless central European one common to urban hubs of that region in the earlier part of the century and therefore in itself not rare enough for anyone to wish to write much about: the browbeating father dominating the others with harsh commands and sarcastic criticism, but no less the domestic despot when ensconced in his heavy chair glowering in sullen silence over one of his several newspapers or over nothing at all—it was as though he could scarcely think of anything else to give voice to other than his blunt demands and abrasive faultfinding; the mother entirely his own creation, spineless, subordinate, and obedient, and therefore unknowable. His sister, the second child of the two, had bided her time in cautious dread while growing up until wisely spotting where the true power in the household lay and then ever since had insinuated herself up to the approval of the father for self-protection, gifts, and privilege. A factor exacerbating the latent discord ingrained in Gregg's central European family life was the anachronistic circumstance that the members did not in fact dwell in metropolitan central Europe, in Kafka's Prague, for instance, or Freud's Vienna, but in midtown Manhattan, in New York City, and were therefore without the customary servant girl and family cook toiling out of view in back, and that the time in which they were living was not the earlier half of the century but the very present, now. It is not a simple task in modern Manhattan to sweep a living bug out of an apartment in a multidwelling building and down into the street without attracting the attention and eliciting the comment of others living there or of staff members at work in the hallways and lobby, but in time they succeeded in doing just that. So there Gregg was, swept cruelly from his house in his weird new incarnation out onto one of the tough sidewalks of New York.

Needless to say, he was surprised.

His unexpected metamorphosis into a homeless insect was not something to which he had ever devoted thought in the calculations of foreseeable calamities he was accustomed to formulating. Gregg, a financial actuary in an executive position of some importance, was an upright, moral soul who never did wrong—he would not even take bribes, and colleagues in the executive offices of the manufacturing firm for which he worked were uneasy with him over that failing and held themselves discreetly aloof, sensing danger from someone of such antiseptic rectitude—and one who customarily took preening pride in anticipating and providing against all sorts of adverse potentials. But this occurrence was one for which he had never made preparation.

He could not think where to begin.

He had to wonder how his fiancée, Felicia, would take to these changes. Felicia was a fastidious woman with principles as strict as his own, and the two were, or had been, perfectly suited. He had been hoping, in fact, that both of them might even try having sex together one day shortly after they were married. Now he was not so sure they would. It seemed to him she might not want to.

Cast out and alone, Gregg began taking stock of himself, looking himself over, so to speak. He counted six legs, three, placed opposite the others, on either side of him, a distribution that was good for balance, and his body felt spliced into a unit of three segmented parts, so he at least knew he was a genuine, purebred insect and not a mere ordinary creeping or flying pest undiscriminating people thought of as insects, like a louse or a worm. Probably he was a beetle of some sort, for nature, or God, as some Victorian naturalist had said, must have loved beetles indeed to have created so many hundreds of thousands of different kinds. Gregg flexed his feelers with a little bit of pride and discovered he enjoyed the muscular sensation. He wondered for a moment or two whether he was perhaps an orange-spotted ladybug, a male ladybug, of course. Responding to an instinct he doubted had been his before, he sensed, then confirmed, with a prickly feeling of imminent danger, that the swarthy uniformed doorman, who was positioned but a few paces away, was eyeing him fixedly with a look of wicked antipathy. Oh, shit, Gregg thought, and with frantic haste went scuttling away on all fours, or all sixes rather, toward the building and buried himself in some clumps of dry leaves and dust heaped up by wind into the dusty crook where the stones of the building met the pavement of the sidewalk. There he paused in hiding to catch his breath after his short flight to safety and to fasten on a course of action.

Where could he go?

He had some doubt Felicia would be eager to welcome him if he made himself known to her in his present appearance. And certainly he could not hope to go back home in the insect form he was inhabiting. He'd been amply warned he'd be risking violent death.

Gregg had, he realized, no idea how to subsist in the city as an insect, although he judged from personal experience as a resident that thousands upon thousands of them did manage to live there happily and thrive. In melancholy moods, in which all his life he frequently had found himself, he had speculated what it might be like to be forced to exist as someone less fortunate. But this was not merely less fortunate. And he had no more idea how to live in the city as a bug of some sort than he would have had as a black in a black neighborhood had he been turned suddenly into an African-American, or as a bag lady with no decent dwelling place in which to shelter herself, or as someone suddenly homeless without savings or income who had to exist on welfare or charity, or in a makeshift haven in some hidden cavity. There were, he'd been told by newspapers, thousands upon thousands of such beings doomed to live out their last days in that impoverished and debased state. In such spells of gloomy, guilt-ridden musing he had tried to visualize himself tragically transported into unlikely pitiful circumstances of that specific sort. How to cope, how would he cope? Who would you turn to if you were suddenly without money and unconnected to anyone who has any, or if all your life you've been white and suddenly you find yourself in the streets as a black? Or you have to live like a bag lady or a man who's homeless, and you've had no experience at that and have no colleagues to train you?

All his life Gregg had been the lucky beneficiary of money in the family, and presently he was, or had been, more than content to be working for a Wall Street manufacturing firm whose sole business activity was manufacturing money. What do you say if suddenly you have no money and no source from which to get any? To whom? But this being changed into an insect was worse, wasn't it? Much worse. Or so it seemed to him, now that it was he, and not someone else, who was the one submerged into his squalid predicament. Not once in all his imagined and occupational analyses as an adult human being and financial actuary had he ever tried to plot how he or any other well-educated person might survive in metropolitan New York as an insect, although now and then he had playfully been called a creep. In dreams he preferred not to recall or discuss with anybody, he had more than once been unendurably mortified, sullied, degraded, terrorized by instances of sexual ill fortune, by clogged, overflowing toilet bowls and the like, and by ferocious pursuit by malignant, powerful men, but this was worse. Once in a whimsical fantasy he had daydreamed the script for a horror movie in which a lone American in a foreign country, himself, having stepped off the train for a quick edible purchase from a platform peddler, watches with shock as the conveyance pulls away with all his papers and the rest of his money aboard, leaving him penniless and without proof of identity in a place in which he did not know the language and no one around spoke his. He had not advanced much deeper than that into the sequence of events because so petrifying was the premise that he was at a loss to proceed. But this surely was worse. Gregg had to wonder again if Felicia would pitch in to help were he to go to her now in her place of business and try to tell her who he was. He thought she might not, even if he were indeed a male ladybug. And how could he go about revealing his identity? He began to think about that. He was not sure he could speak or speak English, and he was missing the physical members to write.

Lacking alternative destinations, he made up his mind and he doggedly and fatalistically started out on the long walk downtown toward the financial district and his office with the manufacturing firm of Goldman Sucks & Company. At Goldman Sucks there were the innumerable snaking tentacles of secret influence that extended always into many bureaus in the White House and maybe wiggled their veiled way even into the very heart of biological nature itself and could effect the genetic reorganization back to the original he thought might be required to remedy the injury of which he was now the hapless victim.

He'd had no breakfast, Gregg remembered as he crawled downtown keeping close to buildings and as far from the footfalls of pedestrians as he could. Nearing a corner with a street vendor from whose large cart the aroma of coffee steamed in a sumptuous cloud, he was abruptly assailed by cramping pangs of hunger. He inhaled the fragrance of Italian sausage too. With a motion intuitive and vestigial, he stretched a hind leg back toward his right hip to make certain he had brought his wallet with cash with him. He would have smiled at the failure if he'd had the facial muscles to do that, or the face. Had he found the wallet with money for the coffee he would not have been able to extract it from the pocket, if he'd had the pocket. Had he found the cash to pay for the coffee, he would not have been able to hold it. If he'd paid for the coffee he would not have been able to drink it, and that was just as well. Probably, he'd drown or scald himself to death inside the cup. Life as a bug, he began to understand, was for him going to prove more confounding than he had at first perceived. An inquisitive soul by nature and occupation, Gregg normally would have greeted with good spirit the opportunity to experience how the other half of the animal world lived. This was not the time. Now he was famished and growing more desperate.

A block or so on he came to some stacks of refuse placed out on the street for pickup. He made his way inside a large corrugated carton he found near a trash can and there he ate some glue. The taste was better than he'd supposed and the glue seemed nutritious, so arriving a little while later at another pile of trash, he went inside another cardboard box and licked some more. A crowd of agitated dark ants scrambled together in a corner to converse nervously about him. There were growing numbers of them and he thought it best to move on. A little while later a roach came crawling up right alongside him to look him over balefully. Gregg hurried past. The roach was brown and ugly. In a mirrored tile he passed he observed that he was not after all a male ladybug as he'd hoped but all brown too and just as ugly. He labored onward toward his chosen destination, avoiding pigeons and fearing wasps, on the alert for carnivorous birds who might, he feared, have found him a treat. By some miracle he overcame all dangers and eventually dragged himself up to the entrance of the Goldman Sucks Building. Luckily, he caught sight of a friend and colleague, Sandy Smith, pausing for a last puff on a cigarette before entering the revolving door. Furtively, Gregg stole near and, attaching himself to the cuff of Smith's trousers, tucked himself inside. Smith was none the wiser. That made easier and less hazardous the journey into the lobby and up in the elevator to his floor. He rode along with Sandy into the offices past the reception area. There he dropped himself off in the wing containing his own office, crept past the secretary he shared with two colleagues—she was again talking on the telephone to her mother; she was always, it seemed, talking on the telephone to her mother, and he wished he had nerve enough to broach to his colleagues the subject of firing her—and inched his way laboriously into his own office, which was of course empty. There he heaved a giant sigh of relief and paused, wondering what to do next. The best course he could decide on was to keep out of sight in some safe place for the while, at least until he could decide on something better to do. Strenuously, then, he labored his way up the leg of his desk and, after looking miserably about, wormed his way inside the telephone console, already planning whom he might call when he could, if he could. It was easy to decipher the contacts; he had only to hop about from one to the other to select the digits he remembered. He was exhausted from his long walk downtown and the ascent up his desk. The shell on his back weighed a ton. He lay down to rest. No sooner had he settled himself into a comfortable position inside the phone unit on a hammock between the wires and their contacts than he heard people burst noisily into his office and human voices he immediately recognized. There were two, Mel and Irv, fellow executive employees with whom he often worked in association, with offices adjacent to his own. Gregg held his breath, fearful of issuing even the slightest sound.

"He's still not here," he heard one say.

"Well, it's probably better without him," replied the other. "You know Gregg. He'd probably raise a million objections and try to stop us from continuing. This way we'll just go ahead without him and say he agreed. He probably wouldn't like the whole idea. This is not his kind of thing."

"What makes him that way? Such a straitlaced prick?" Gregg quivered.

"The genes, I think. It must be in the genes."

"Don't we all have the same genes?"

"I don't know, it's not what I specialize in. He must have a different one. Or maybe he's missing one, like having a screw loose. Anyway, we've got his letterhead and his appointment book, and his initials are easy to copy. We'll underwrite the bond issue the way we talked about it. Even though they'll probably turn out to be worthless."

"Isn't that unethical?"

"Sure. But that's not our specialty either. We're in the business of manufacturing money. That's why we're here. And this deal will manufacture a lot, for us."

"And you're sure they're worthless?"

"They're Russian government bonds. What do you think? That's why we can get to handle the issue at such a good price. Then we unload them fast in big bunches on our best institutional clients. The company makes its big profit. And we get our big bonus. That's all money in the bank long before the bonds turn to plain paper."

"Don't they mind, the ones we dump them on?"

"Nah. They're big and they can afford it. They know they can't win all the time. They can take a joke. Also, by the time they find out we'll probably both be working for other companies at better jobs. Let's run with it while Gregg is not here and we've still got the chance to bypass him."

"What about Gus?"

"Gus?"

"How will he feel when he finds out? Will he disapprove?"

"Oh, you know Gus. Gus is a cagey old fox who never wants to hear about anything he might disapprove of, just as long as we keep manufacturing money for the company. And that's just what we'll be doing. Gus might never find out. If he does find out, he might not disapprove. And if he does disapprove, we'll just lay all the blame on Gregg and pretend we didn't know anything about the ins and outs of it. Okay?"

"Sounds great to me."

Gregg was ready to explode in protest. He had not much minded being ticketed as straitlaced—he took a compliment from that one—but he'd bristled at hearing himself called a prick. Now he could not—though he tried—contain himself.

"Hey, you guys, you just wait a minute!" he shouted irately from inside the telephone console—his face flushing, or what he had in place of a face flushing—as loudly and as masterfully as he could. Despite the effort, his voice, lacking a large sound chamber for booming amplification, came out thin, little more than a spoken squeak.

And Mel and Irv responded in unison to each other in instant confusion.

"What'd you say?" they both said to the other.

"Didn't you just say something?" they asked in reply.

"No, I thought you did," said both.

"No, I didn't," said one before the other.

"Okay," said the other. "We're set. Now let's get the hell out of here in case that straitlaced prick does show up."

"Sure."

Gregg's first reaction was to chase after them. They were gone before he could even begin to untangle all his legs from the various nubs and the filaments of wires. When at last he was loose, he acted quickly to telephone Gus. He had a voice, he knew the extension number, and he popped about from one connection point to another. His secretary, fortunately, was still absorbed on the phone with her mother. But Gus, as they'd described him, was indeed a cagey old fox who never wanted to see or hear about anything of which he might disapprove, a wise old owl who consequently was seldom in for Gregg. He was not in for him now.

Failing there, Gregg took the most plausible action he could think of: he phoned his physician to describe his condition and obtain a remedy.

But someone must have been telling lies about his physician, for overnight, without having done anything else wrong, he had been transformed into an earwig.

Gregg next called his psychotherapist: someone must have been telling lies about her too, for without having done anything wrong, she'd been changed into a mockingbird.

In succession he tried his lawyer, his congressman, and his senator, but someone must have been telling lies about them too, or the truth, for they had been turned into a leech, a mite, and an exotic parasite.

He next tried the White House, but someone must have been telling the truth about the president too, for overnight he had emerged groggily from an anxious sleep as a chameleon.

In utter desperation, Gregg tried his spiritual adviser.

But someone must have been telling lies about his spiritual adviser too.

And Franz Kafka had been absolutely right in ending his long short story exactly where he did, Pota saw, instead of where Pota thought for a while he could take it, ending it as a tragedy for the bug, who gives up the ghost and dies in his room, and with a happy ending for the rest of the family, who flower when at last liberated from the disgrace he embodied for them.

But Kafka was a modest, inhibited author in Prague neurotically reluctant to have almost any of his work published, and not a rank-conscious American author like Eugene Pota, one of many and typical of all, who craved with each new production, though elevated, demanding, and artistically intellectual rather than merely fascinating, to achieve what in his country was known as a massive, mass-market best-seller that would make a big blockbuster of a movie and win for him more than two million dollars.

For dinner that night, Pota replied when Polly asked, he thought he might like something with Italian sausage, maybe sausage and peppers. Polly went shopping and that's what he ate. He was tired of glue. She didn't know what he was talking about when he made mention of that.

He did not take time to tell her.

Was he wanting too much? he wondered. Of the authors he admired, how many had died rich, had enjoyed even one big, mass-market best-seller that was turned into a blockbuster of a movie and had gained from it more than two million dollars?

Not Kafka. Certainly not Melville or Dostoyevsky, who had both struggled in penury. Not Mark Twain, who'd known some wealth and then heavy debt, heavy debt and domestic tragedy. With the thought of Mark Twain, an idea for a new approach to Tom Sawyer streaked through his mind. He set it aside for the future. Instead he thought, with bitterness, of making a quick list of writers who had luxuriated in secure, comfortable affluence throughout their lives, guessing with foresight there'd be only few. He moved through his memory to names in the biographical data he'd been collecting for his speech on the literature of despair he was soon due to give. When he could not think of even a single one with which to top his list, he abandoned the idea and sat back in a smoldering fury.

He was angry and dissatisfied with himself. He felt mean, spiteful, and malevolent, furtive and devious. *Spleen* was the word he thought of in description. He nursed with spleen the hopeful, masochistic wish that Polly would do something annoying just for the pleasurable relief he might enjoy of losing his temper and barking at her. But Polly, who, except when languishing in a sulk of her own, was more magnanimous and sensitive than his earlier wives, perceived his mood and benevolently kept her distance. He felt physically ill, as though something noxious was seeping from his liver or his heart, and he wanted a fight.

He wanted a book. He had an idea. He had an opening. He loved his title.

Spleen

Call me Gene.

I am a mean Gene . . . spiteful . . . malevolent and sneaky too. I gorge myself on spleen. I keep my real self hidden, dwell underground, where hardly anyone can spy me. I'm not always at my best, my constitution is not always what it should be, but that doesn't disturb me, and I don't care. I don't see a doctor. When I'm not feeling my best, I sometimes injure others, do wicked things. I assert my bad nature in different sly and spiteful ways. I'll pitch in with others in a malignant band to ruin someone early, and that's not always a good thing. Or is it? Aren't there too many people? Aren't there always too many?

Sure, there are. Look at the past. Look at what's going on now. Those that can't survive shouldn't survive, and don't in the long run, do they?

We get together, me and my gang, and encourage large numbers of normal, virtuous, awful people to murder and do awful things to large numbers of other virtuous, awful people, and to women and very young people too. And to carry on killing and maiming that way with a conviction of justice and without compunction, with pleasure, pride, and a complacent sense of righteous accomplishment.

Examples?

Easy.

Just look today at Africa, Europe, Asia, at England, and at America—once I started a list, I could never complete it. I could begin just about anywhere in the world, always. I could start with almost any human civilization we know about, and I would never, never be able to finish, for the evil, savage things civilized, bad-natured men and women do to other men and women continue to outrace the faculty of anyone to make note of them all.

We see to that.

Bad nature is human nature.

We see to that too.

I know what I'm talking about.

I'm old, and I've been just about everywhere and seen almost everything. I was right there with the writer Dostoyevsky through all his epileptic fits and other chaotic miseries and helped him drive his underground man underground, with all the wretched envy and projected, self-destructive spite consuming him from within. With Tolstoy too. Here's a laugh. Tolstoy hated crowds of admirers, hated his wife—and the old writer collapsed in a train station while fleeing his home and lived just long enough for crowds of journalists and dignitaries to collect and for his wife to arrive for him to watch her watching him die. We did more with Gogol. We drove him crazy and gave him a horrifying fear of leeches. Suicidal, he tried to starve himself to death, then stab himself to death, and, dying, found himself covered with leeches by doctors seeking to prolong his life. Pushkin perhaps came to an easier end, the beloved Russian poet killed in a duel at thirty-eight by an amoral adventurer who'd openly and audaciously gone chasing after his flirtatious wife, leaving Pushkin no choice but to challenge. Troubled Dostoyevsky had never in his turbulent life known much peace and quiet or financial security. When he had money, he gambled it away; when he wrote a book, he rewrote, and reorganized, and restarted, and reorganized again more times than any scholar then or since enjoyed keeping track of.

You find funny these ironies.

We make sure you do.

Here's more. Maxim Gorky fled for his life into exile under the rule of the tsars; under the rule of the communists, Isaac Babel was sent to prison and disappeared.

The world has never been good to Russian authors, least of all other Russians.

Believe it or not—I don't care if you do or don't—I was right there with Jonah and in the whale. On the spot too with Herman Melville and his whale, at the crest of his success and then with him and his white whale—call him Moby-Dick—and his pathetic decline into poverty and oblivion—Melville's, not Moby's, precipitated by his preoccupation with that same white whale of his, which did as much figurative damage to the author and his literary status as to anyone else. If you agree there was a Captain Ahab and a Moby-Dick, then you have to agree I was right there with them, with both, with each, right up to the end. Which one would you guess I was rooting for? I'll bet you're wrong. I sided with neither one. I had no feeling for either one. I have no feelings.

I am older than you are and I know what I'm saying.

We were born the same time, you and I, to the minute, for that matter, but I was there before you were, long before, and I am older than you are and I know much more. Even though we were born together. I am older than everyone you know and older than everyone you can imagine, but I'm fresh as a daisy, almost always.

I was there when they crucified your Lord.

I was there with him, and I was down there with the Roman soldiers, with every one of them, in every fiber of their being, and with every one of the onlookers too, the males and the females, the adults and the children. I was part of all of them, a pretty good part. I took no sides. And I was older than all of them, in this world before they were. And none of them suspected, not man, woman, or child, that they were reacting to the experience the way they had to, no matter which faction they were favoring: that they were feeling the only way they could, the way we prompted them to, that they as thinking, feeling, contemplating, individual, highly developed human beings were merely mechanisms of the brain, over which they had never for a second had an iota of control, and that never ever in their lives would they have even an instant of free will, not one moment of choice.

The brain decides, not the individual that encases it.

Believe it or not—you won't—but I am older than Methuselah. Way older. Yes, sir. And if man really was created in God's image, then I had to be there with Adam too, as old as he was if not older, and with Eve, naked and fig leafed, maybe even before—if the animals were created first, I was there in the

113

garden of Eden sooner than these first parents were—and older than they were. Today too, I am everywhere at once and always in the same place.

I bet you've got it now.

Sure. A gene. Always in the same spot on the same chromosome, the identification doesn't matter, you wouldn't remember it anyway, and I'm in every cell in your body and in everyone else's (maybe not in every ovum and sperm cell—I couldn't swear to that) and in a large number of animals you'd recognize too and would not like being so closely related to.

It's pretty crowded down here on my chromosome and up here where all of us always are. Not exactly cheek by jowl, I'd have to say, because we have no cheeks and have no jowls, but one on top of the other in ladder style, thousands and thousands of us crammed in place between these spiraling bonds of DNA holding us in fixed position, but by now we've learned to live with each other, and we get along comfortably and work with each other in rigid regularity, with little conflict, and we've been there together for everything you know about or can imagine.

Napoleon? Sure. With Josephine? Why not? With his other women too. That Napoleon was a very funny fellow in a very funny France. He won battles and lost campaigns and kept failing upward until he could declare himself emperor. Julius Caesar? Of course. I was right there with Caesar on the Ides of March, and even before, when he crossed the Rubicon with his lawless big ideas that bore him to victory and led to his ruin, and even before that. I was at his side when he was assassinated, and in his side too, when he said, *"Et tu, Brute?"* And I was with Brutus too when he struck with his own knife and Caesar decided to lie down and die, especially when all of us gave him no choice. But not me, I lived on; he died, but I lived on. If not in him then in everyone else. I always live on, if you call what I do living. I was alive and well in all of the others, undamaged, unchanged, exactly the same. Not really alive. I'm never what you would call alive. I'm just a string of molecules. But I function, I do my job, I do what I have to do, I have no choice either, and I help make you do what you have to, whether you like it or not, whether you even *know* it or not, and by now I've seen and heard just about everything. I was in Egypt in bed with Caesar and Cleopatra. I know exactly what Cleopatra said and did in that bed that was new to Caesar the first time she lay with him and each time after, and I know the dozens of variations she practiced on Marc Antony years later too, when she was even better, and he gave up everything. I'd like to let you in on it if I could. But I can't say a word. All in all it's been a pretty exciting time, and a funny one too, from our point of view.

For instance, none of those gawky people feeling proud as peacocks to be invited to sleep in the Lincoln room of Clinton's White House in return for their large payments to the Democratic Party ever seemed to suspect the microphone in the room conveying their conversation to amused listeners, who often could not keep their faces straight when they were all together the next day. It was enough to make me laugh out loud. But I can't do that. I can't laugh. Better than an X-rated movie, how dignified, successful men and women will talk and what they will try to do when they fall to it like insects and other animals. It was a truth soon universally acknowledged that every couple there, regardless of age or physical infirmity, no matter how intensely they had grown to abhor each other in normal circumstances, felt the need, the positive obligation, to fall to it with what sexual practices remained active to them on the venerated occasion of that unforgettable night they spent in the famed Lincoln room of the White House. It was a duty, a patriotic responsibility. It was often remarked by presidential insiders that the Lincoln room of the White House was a good place to get laid, a sure thing. And there was a dominating compulsion to let go and talk dirty and say shitty things in the Lincoln bedroom of the White House—after all, they did not know when they would ever have another chance to talk dirty and say shitty things in so lofty a venue. I was inside on the mattress with them, with both of them, and outside with the elite corps of eavesdroppers. Oh, the things I could tell you, if I could only talk. But I can't talk, so I can't tell.

I can only smell. Smell things, not give off odors. That's my function, my job. I'm a mere olfactory receptor, and I do that work along with about a thousand others who all pitch in together to do the same thing. How else do you think you do it? We smell things for you. I can smell a rat for you and I can smell bullshit too. And there's more than enough, more than I want to smell, of both in the capital cities of what people in government like to call the two-party democracies, especially in Washington, and in London too. I know everything. I'm everywhere all the time, and I know what happened in those eighteen minutes of—surprise—missing conversation on the Nixon tapes and I know how they were erased. You should have heard what all those people in the White House really said when they talked in secrecy about settling in Vietnam, the Johnsonites and the Nixonites. It was enough to make me vomit, but I can't vomit. It's not my specialty. I can tell you what every president and his wife talked about when they thought they were alone and what every president and his mistress talked about when the wife was away. I was with Lee Harvey Oswald the day Kennedy was killed, and I was with Marilyn Monroe the day she died and know all that happened, and the day before, and the day before too. I could really write a book. Oh, could I write a mean, spiteful, evil book about Marilyn and everything and everyone else you might have admired and wondered about, spill mean, spiteful secrets you never suspected about every venerable public figure you've ever looked up to, secrets that are odious and repugnant, disgusting. Oh, could I write a book!

But . . . I can't write.

And I can't write either, expostulated the elderly author, Eugene Pota, laughing sardonically with a sensation of woe, no, positively cannot write a novel about a gene resting passively on a chromosome like a fucking fly on a wall, merely hearing and reporting things other characters are doing and playing no true role in any of them. And this gene I'm inventing may be able to smell a rat and a load of bullshit, but he's full of bullshit too. He may be there in every cell in every human being, but he's not the same one—physically the individual same one—in every person everywhere all the time—he couldn't be, he'd have to be everywhere at once all the time, communicating with all the others all the time, and he'd surely be crushed by an information overload, wouldn't he? And he couldn't have been eavesdropping on Marilyn Monroe in her bedroom in California and scheming with Lee Harvey Oswald in Russia or Texas and with me off on a summer vacation at Fire Island when she died, and if I can figure that out now, thought Eugene Pota, everyone else will be able to smell a rat too and know right off that I'm full of bullshit too. He can't talk and he can't write, but what is it he's doing? Talking and writing—so the hell with that one also. What was I thinking of? The hell with neo-Darwinism as a formative precept, and with evolutionary determinism too, to the appalling—but unanswerable—idea that everything we do has to be done, every choice we make has already been chosen, that everything we think we decide has already been programmed in the brain, even as I am deciding right now, decided Eugene Pota, down to the very last word I write, even to the changing of that word with the substitution of another.

Who wants to read about that?

I must have a hero with choice, Pota told himself again in an unvoiced wail, a decent protagonist, a man or a boy or a woman in trouble who has—or thinks he has—free will and has to cause or ward off danger and make things happen. He'd known that all along, he reminded himself. That was one of the weaknesses of God in his idea *God's Wife*. He'd be passive, the butt of jokes. Pota needed a plot moved along by people who *do* things. Interesting characters, if not necessarily heroic, at least strong, decisive figures who make things happen.

He shoved these sheets about a gene away into a file in his drawer. And with a sublime feeling of exhilarating release, he again brought out the older one with the idea that all along had been maturing more auspiciously in his deliberations. He laughed again. His recess into vacillation was over. Decisively, he made up his mind to make up his mind, and he made up his mind and printed out this title page:

A SEXUAL BIOGRAPHY
OF MY WIFE

A New Novel

by

Eugene Pota

Pota remembered very little about the duke of Marlborough. That he was not the duke of Wellington was just about all. And knew nothing at all about the duchess, apart from the quote come upon more than once that her lord had come home from the wars one night and pleasured her twice with his boots on. A passing effort at finding out more about her turned up only another statement from somewhere to the effect that she knew nothing about books, only about cards and men. This was a promising start for a female character in a humorous and erotic novel to be a sexual biography of somebody's wife. But pondering further and more deeply about her initial comment, Pota began to be puzzled more and more by that second time of her lord's pleasuring her with the boots on. Was there not a period of repose in between? If only for the catching of breath? Why had he not taken off his boots in the interval? Unless he was one of those priapic men one hears about who are hard again before they are completely dry from the first time. Perhaps it was he, Marlborough, and not the duke of Wellington, as Pota for so many years might mistakenly have believed, who was known also as the Iron Duke. And where were his trousers both those times? Could military trousers in late eighteenth or early nineteenth century England be removed with the boots still on? Did men wear belts and suspenders then, and what were suspenders and belts called? And what about the rest of his linen, and hers? What was their linen? Could it be explained, perhaps, Pota the novelist had to wonder, that an English gentleman, especially one who'd been a victorious general, could not or would not deign to remove his boots himself, no matter the occasion, and that he was reluctant to summon his man or her maid into milady's bedroom in those private circumstances in which his trousers were or had been down about his ankles and his boots? Would the duchess not stoop so low as to remove his boots for him? Would he permit her to?

There was much, Pota saw with a sinking heart, that he would have to find out, and Pota abhorred doing research. He was sure that Wellington—or was it Marlborough?—had a favorite mistress—maybe this was true of both—the wife of an acquiescent male who doubtless had at least one intimate lady friend of his own. After all, what else were aristocratic women in England for? No, the mistress of the male friend probably would not have been the wife of Wellington, or Marlborough. That would have been too neat, and decadent. And one of them, maybe Wellington, perhaps Marlborough, was embarrassingly involved with a second woman bent on blackmail who threatened to make things known to all with a published account of their carnal exercises. Publish and be damned, said Marlborough. Or was it Wellington? She did both, according to the anecdote. She did publish, and was damned by most for having done so. One of them—Marlborough or Wellington, not both, maybe both—was Blenheim, an ancestor of our Winston Churchill, inducing Churchill, our Churchill, to remark, when complimented on the richness of his genealogical descent: Yes, but look at all those that came in between.

Pota in the first flush of his preliminary enthusiasms recalled the advice about sex by Lord Chesterfield to his son, figures of that time who might comfortably appear in his book, that the pleasure was momentary, the position ridiculous, and the expense exorbitant. He jotted this down on one of his three-by-five note cards, in fear he might overlook his inspired intent to use it.

Pota pondered further about the preparations Marlborough, or Wellington, was required by custom to undergo before calling upon his, or their, mistress, at the contrast between the fixed formality of attire and speech and the vigorous and animalistic lewdness that was the purpose of their call and their coming together in amatory violence to make the beast with two backs. Now he had Shakespeare to make use of too, even though the duchess maintained she knew nothing of books. Pota knew plenty and would not be easily deterred from making use of what he knew. But that contrast began to bother him, along with that difference between what he did not know and what he did know, or what could be readily imagined. Pota did not know the names for the articles of clothing they wore, for the food and drink they favored, the furnishings in the home. He was pretty sure he still knew the difference between a bodkin, a jerkin, and a firkin, but that was about all, and he began to balk at the prospect of having to find out more. He tried to imagine the propriety of the dialogue between them on these sojourns for sexual ravishment.

"Please, sir, if Your Lordship does not mind, would Your Lordship move himself up upon me a little higher? You are crushing my chest and I am finding difficulty in breathing."

"As you wish, milady. And please do me the honor of digging your fingernails into the cheeks of my arse instead of allowing your hands to lie there so uselessly."

And that did it for Pota. That word *arse*. It was that word *arse* that made him change his mind. Not to save his life was he going to embark on a book in which for a good old American word like *ass* he would have to substitute a quaintly exotic one like *arse*.

It was in a merry mood of making considerable progress that he came to the express, irreversible decision to return to his original idea of writing a sex book, perhaps more than vaguely pornographic, from the point of view of a contemporary American woman, as told by a man, perhaps even by a man like himself, who was trying to write a sex book from the point of view of a woman, as he himself was now in fact actually doing. And then he was jolted to another halt.

He understood, for perhaps the first time in his life, that he did not know much more about the women of his own day then he did about the duchess of Marlborough, knew not nearly enough, and hardly anything about their sexuality, if they had such a thing, and he knew that most did. They fantasized too, they also had longings, especially when young. But what did they think about when they thought only to themselves, and with what vocabulary? His barbed retort to Polly awhile back about a woman sitting down to urinate now grew for him into an item of essential knowledge. How did a woman's breasts feel—he knew how a woman's breasts felt to him, but how did they feel to her, when she was alone, when she dressed, when she turned over in her sleep? When she went jogging? These were things he would have to know. Polly would be uncomfortable if he inquired of her, and he would be uncomfortable too. Did normal, ordinary women talk to each other about sex as sex, the way men did? He guessed young girls did, openly and bluntly, as never before. He had known young girls who did, talked to him and to their close girlfriends with him present, until they'd graduated decorously into marriage and onward into middle age, until he no longer was in touch with them.

He had to wonder: did they, women, think of sex as often as he did, on numerous occasions every day, with comparable mental images? He very much doubted that. He doubted most other men thought about it as often as he did.

The mothers in marriages of younger couples were carting their teenage daughters off to gynecologists for birth control devices even before they left secondary school and went away to college. What did these very young girls talk about, boast about, in their locker rooms and shower rooms, on their toilet seats, privately in their dormitories? He could guess, but he wanted to be sure. He had a pretty sound idea they now talked about sex as effusively as males did, if not more, and in a language more crude. Were women affected favorably by the size of a large penis? Sure they were. Of course they were. They had to be, if they were into sex at all.

He remembered from a brief friendship between marriages talking to a Southern girl who startled him on the phone one morning when he called by exclaiming in a rapture: "Oh, God, it's such a beautiful day outside, I feel like fucking the whole world!"

Probably, that was the first time he'd heard that word from the mouth of a woman, and certainly the first time he'd heard that verb used in an active, rather than a passive, voice when referring to a female. When they were together that afternoon, he amused himself with the notion that she in her mind was doing to him, the author, what he in his mind was doing to her, the liberated photographer's model. That, he supposed now, was an indication of the new equality of the sexes, and he was still not sure that he liked it.

He made lists of questions he'd want the answers to about women's sexual experiences from preadolescence through menopause and beyond. When they were complete and in chronological sequence, he read them through once more on the screen of his word processor and then guiltily, in shuddering haste, erased them all, leaving not one note. They read unmistakably, even to him, like queries evoked by the pathological curiosity of a degenerate voyeur, and he wondered, uneasily, if that was perhaps what they unconsciously had been.

He thought of an old friend now in Florida he knew he could talk to frankly and find out certain things, a woman he had not seen in perhaps fifteen years. But in contacting a different friend in New York for her current phone number, he was horrified to find out that the year before she'd been burned very badly from the waist down in a boating accident and had been in an intensive care unit for something like six weeks before it was certain she would survive. He called her in Key West right away, forgetting his original purpose.

"I just found out about it from Michelle. Oh, Pattie, my darling, I'm so sorry, I'm all broken up."

"That was all over more than a year ago," she consoled him cheerfully. Part of her continual loveliness was that she could always be cheerful about everything, and had been cheerful in the hospital too when she was not in pain or sedated. "The medical part's finished. And I've just collected my big settlement money from the insurance company, so I'm well off for a while and can afford to start writing magazine articles again. Gene, I'm so glad you called. It's good to be talking to you."

"No more pain?"

"No, but you should see what I look like from the hips down."

"I want to."

"No, you don't. I'm never going to go to a beach again or wear shorts or anything, just caftans and muumuus. I told my doctor that from now on I'm only going to give blow jobs. She's a woman from Finland and she didn't know what to make of me."

"She didn't know how good you are at it. No more tango? Are you still crazy about the tango?"

"How did you know about that?"

"You wrote about it in that last collection of magazine pieces you published a few years ago. I sent you a fan letter after I bought the book. Don't you remember?"

"Oh, Gene, I do love you. No, I haven't tangoed since the accident. I spent a fortune doing that."

"And I love you. I've never stopped. I'm going to start making some plans and find some way to come down to see

129

you for a few days. We'll lie down together and drink some scotch."

"I don't drink. I haven't had a drink in fifteen years, not since AA. Have you forgotten that part?"

"Then I'll have some scotch, while you give me a blow job."

"Or ten. You won't want to look at me."

"Yes, I do."

"It's ghastly."

"So what? It's only skin, Pattie. It isn't you. You know what it looks like now, don't you? You may not like it but you've gotten used to it. It happened. You live with your sister, you have a maid, they're used to it. They don't cringe anymore, do they? And neither do you. You've got a boyfriend?"

"A good one this time, I think."

"He's used to you too, I'll bet. I'll be appalled the first time I see you and touch your legs. I'll look again. I'll know what's there. And that's all there is to it. And we'll both be the same. Except that my hands now shake a bit."

"Call me again tomorrow, or the next day, or the next. I want to keep talking to you."

"I'm not due for anything in Florida for a while," he said when he did phone the next day. "But I'll think something up and get down there soon. I want to see you. I want very much to be with you for a while."

"Hurry up. I spoke to Adele yesterday and told her you called." It was Pattie who'd introduced those two a long time back and helped bring them together. "She wonders why you never call to talk to her."

"Does she?" Pota pursed his lips, pausing while he thought. "She's still married, isn't she?"

"Yes. Two daughters. Both away in school now, I think."

"I've never called her because I know I'll fall in love with her again if I did talk to her," Pota answered, prizing his reply. "And I don't want to have to go through another divorce again. Tell her I said that. She'll be complimented to hear it that way."

"I'll bet she will," said Pattie. "That's one of the sweetest lies I've ever heard."

Pota felt good about himself and then not quite so good about this new turn of events. Polly would be hurt if he went to Florida to see another woman, and she didn't deserve that. But he would be denied if he didn't go, and he didn't deserve that either. His course was clear.

He would have to lie. It had worked before with his other wives.

He stretched himself out on his bed in his studio to grapple with the details of this new spree he was plotting and was soon thinking of other things and very soon after that he was sound asleep in another nap.

Once tempted out of the cautious pattern of prudent rectitude in which he dutifully had confined himself since his marriage to Polly, he felt an arousing momentum to keep sailing along. He next contacted Louise, the girl, now woman, who'd introduced him to Tantric art far back and failed in her attempts to convert him to vegetarianism and astrology, but that conversation too brought him only more rotten news and no information for help with his sex book. The man she'd been with for close to twenty years was now ailing in a way necessitating periodic hospitalizations for seriously disabling surgery, and she had just that week resigned her executive position in entertainment publicity to have more time to care for him. It was like her to do that. Both very tough and tender too, she was an admirable person of strict principle. At their parting, she had made clear her determination of unfaltering fidelity, which he respected, and she respected that he'd not once attempted to coax her away from it. Now she was excited to hear from him. Not only did she recall the Tantric art when he mentioned it, but still had the posters up in the apartment she'd furnished. Pota had been hoping to meet her discreetly in midtown near her office for lunch or dinner, and then—who could tell what might follow?

"Oh, yeah, Gene, I'd love to see you the next time you're in the city."

"I'll even come downtown, if it's more convenient for you now. We'll have drinks or dinner when you're free and I'm there alone. I'd love to catch up with you."

"Sure," said Louise. "But people recognize you now, don't they?"

"Yes, they often do."

"And I don't want to start any trouble, not for me or for you."

"Neither do I," said Pota, speaking truthfully, but only after grasping her meaning. "We'll make it lunch or coffee. There are things I want to find out and I think you could help."

"And I won't let you up here when he's not around."

"Of course not. Louise, I love you, I've never stopped loving you, and all the friends of mine you ever met still love you. I'm more than seventy-five years old now. I can't pounce anymore. I can love you just by sitting across a table and talking to you, as I'm talking to you right now, and listening to you tell me all that's been happening all these years. Is your sister still married?"

"Oh, yes. That lasted. She's got children, and I'm their happy aunt."

"Your mother okay?"

"In a nursing home. Please do call me when you can. I'd love to see you. I need someone to talk to about all that's happening."

"I'm good at that."

"I know you are. It's not that I feel lonely. I don't feel lonely, I've got friends and things to do, but sometimes now I feel so all alone."

And early that same evening, there came, not entirely by coincidence, the phone call he had daydreamed of occasionally and hoped to put into a novel sometime if ever he was doing one into which it would fit naturally.

"I'm Adele's husband," said the man right off. "She knows I'm calling. She isn't well anymore. She occasionally says she'd like to talk to you at least once more, while she's still able to talk fluently. If I'm calling at an inconvenient time, simply get angry and say so and I'll try again another time."

"Of course it's inconvenient," said Pota brusquely. "We're in the middle of dinner. And I don't have that financial information handy and don't want to look for it right now. Leave me your number and I'll call you at the bank tomorrow." He was irate when he turned to Polly. "These damn banks and their evening telephone solicitations. I swear I'd change if it didn't involve so much paperwork. And any bank I'd change to would probably be just as bad. I wish they'd pass a law against these telephone solicitations."

"What did he want?"

"To switch my savings accounts to ones paying more interest."

His call the next day went not to a bank but a law office.

"It sounds fishy," said Eugene Pota.

"I can see why you feel that." The voice of the man was mellifluous and self-assured, glib. "But it isn't. I promise you."

"Yeah? What is it?"

"It's called ALS. That stands for amyotrophic lateral sclerosis."

"I know that."

"Also known as Lou Gehrig's disease."

"I know that too. Women get it too?"

"She did."

"I'll want to talk to her first."

"Of course. My name is Seymour, by the way, in case you want to be friends."

"When's a good time to phone?"

"Whenever you want to. I work all day, usually late. I'm a lawyer, if you care."

"I know that too. You talk smoothly, like one who negotiates."

"I do that a lot. There's no need to be cross with me, really there isn't."

"I'm not cross with you. I'm angry at the news."

"And I'm usually away all day Saturday and Sunday, if the weather's nice."

"Golf?"

"Adele guessed you'd say that."

"Adele knows people. She's very smart. By now you've found that out."

"Shall I tell her you'll come? Will you come to see her?"

"Of course I will. If she really wants me to. Did you think I'd say no?"

"She wasn't that sure."

"I'd bet you she was."

A young Indonesian maid admitted him into an airy large apartment with many windows overlooking the reservoir in Central Park and facing with an expansive grandeur of its own the Fifth Avenue apartment houses on the other side. Pota would have guessed that if she ever had a maid, she would insist on one that was young and pretty, one she could help mold. She tended to be instructional. With the maid watching, they embraced awkwardly, then held to each other a bit longer and kissed a second time a bit more warmly than is normal for cursory greetings.

"I'm glad you're here," she said.

"So am I."

"You're looking good."

"So are you."

She truly did look much better than he had expected, very much better than he had feared. But she moved somewhat jerkily, it seemed to him, as she walked to reseat herself on a couch, where, he could see, she had been drinking a white wine as she waited. He declined when she offered him a glass. She leaned back in an expansive way he remembered, regarding him through small dark eyes with a look that was suspicious and probing, her mouth shaped in a superior half smile that was already tinged with a glimmer of frisky scorn.

"I've seen your photos now and then. You look much better in person, healthier. You really do look wonderful, considering."

"So do you."

"Healthier too?"

"Yes."

"Sure," she jeered dryly.

"You really do look wonderful."

"Sure."

"You do. In a way that reminds me of your mother."

"My mother?"

"We had lunch together once. Don't you remember? She was aging elegantly. We both agreed. Her hair was turning from an ash blonde to silver, or a shiny platinum, and her skin was golden."

"Tawny, I would call it."

"And so is yours. Is she still with us?"

"No, she's dead. My father's gone too."

He said with a chuckle, "Did they ever get used to you?"

"No." She laughed softly too. "I had to keep them under my thumb all the way. But tell me, Gene," she continued, and calmly leaned back again, displaying deliberately an expression of triumphant mirth, "do you still give great head?"

"What?"

"I'm sure you heard me. Didn't you hear what I said?"

"Sure I did. My exclamation was one of amazement. I'm hard of hearing, but not that hard."

"Well, do you?"

He shrugged and uttered a heavy sigh of resignation. "I don't know. I haven't tried it in a long time."

"Do you want to?"

"What?"

"Again what?"

"When?"

"Now."

"Do you," he countered, "want me to?"

"I don't know." She smiled. "I haven't tried it in a long time either. Do you want to?"

"If you want me to."

"Do you want to?"

"Do you want me to? I've always tried to give you everything you wanted. I drank that brewer's yeast stuff with you for lunch for almost a year. I even went to see a psychic with you when you wanted me to. That was foolish, and dangerous. You didn't tell me a magazine was doing a piece on him."

"I really didn't know. You wouldn't leave your wife for me."

"Except that."

"You left her later anyway."

"No, I didn't. We parted. I didn't want to. It was *not* my idea. And it wasn't over anything like that."

"Would you leave this one for me?"

"No, of course not."

"I wouldn't blame you, considering what's going to happen to me."

"Adele, please don't abuse me. You know that's not the principal reason. And just how long do you think we would have lasted married together, me as your husband and you as my devoted housewife?"

"Not long, I guess. And then, in a very short time, you probably would have had some other girl on your hands, badgering you to leave me."

"And what about you, with other men? But you've been married a long time now too, haven't you?"

"I've loved being married. I really do. I've loved having daughters and bringing them up. And every time I find myself hating it, I just have to remind myself how much I love it. My girls went into sex earlier than I did, and I started pretty young."

"Without encouragement, maternal encouragement?"

"And without discouragement."

"That's one of the things I'm glad to hear from you. I'm trying to write a sex book from the point of view of a woman."

"I've already written one. I couldn't get it published."

"Mine will be. But it isn't working out. So far, there's too much I don't know."

"Use mine."

"That wouldn't work either. And my sex book isn't turning out to be as much fun as I thought it would. Or any fun at all so far. I keep running into bad omens in my research. I may put it aside or give it up altogether and have a crack at a different idea I have in mind." She looked at him, waiting. "Something like a novel about Mark Twain and the life of an American writer."

"Mine hasn't been that successful."

"Neither was his. That would be the point. And mine may be hobbling along to an end, together with very much else I've enjoyed."

"Me?"

"Yes. Of course. What lies ahead for you?"

"I'd rather not say."

"I've been waiting to hear."

She changed the subject. "Your hands shake a little now, don't they?"

He replied with a nod. "I know."

"That's called a tremor," she said.

"I would never have guessed."

"Age?"

"Coffee and whiskey help. But mostly age."

"Mine do too. Do you still listen to Schubert?"

"More often than ever."

"Despite the agitation and the pain?"

"Because of the agitation and the pain. Suddenly, you've been looking so sad, Adele."

She sighed and lowered her gaze. "Everyone's getting so old. And because soon we'll be boring to each other. We're just about all talked out already, aren't we?"

"No, not all," said Pota, again boldly counting himself at that stage of nostalgia in his life in which he honestly could say such things to her as he was about to. "I've never stopped thinking about you, not for long. I've never stopped being in love with you. I'd never felt for anyone the way I felt about you, and I've not felt that way for anyone since, and still do. I doubt I ever will."

She heard him through in somber silence and said, patting the cushion, "Come sit here beside me."

He rose stiffly and crossed the room to join her on the sofa. She extended an outstretched arm to steady him as he turned to seat himself, and he came to rest with his hand inside her thigh. He squeezed gently, rubbing a bit, and left it there. She stared down at his hand a moment. Then, turning in toward him, she reached her arms around his shoulders, and as they settled together against the backrest, she began weeping noiselessly, making not one sound, spilling tears against his neck that felt ice cold.

It's just, he thought, what he might have done, had she not done it first.

"It's just what I would have done," Pota later revealed softly, after she'd recovered and expressed her regret for having let go that way, "if you hadn't done it first."

Smiling, she looked intently into his eyes. "Tell me, Gene, do you ever stop to wonder why women love you?"

Smiling, he shook his head. "No."

TOM SAWYER, NOVELIST

"Tom."

No answer.

"Tom."

No answer.

"Oh, shit," said Aunt Polly. "Where is that boy this time? I hope he hasn't really gone off looking for that Mr. Clemens to learn how to be an author. That would be terrible, terrible, I know it would."

Alas, Tom Sawyer's small valise was gone.

So were a spare shirt, a change of underwear, an extra pair of socks, a comb, a toothbrush, his bamboo fishing pole, and a bar of soap. Pinned to the top of the blanket in his room was a hand-lettered note from Tom Sawyer to Aunt Polly informing her that he had indeed gone off toward Connecticut to find Mr. Samuel Clemens, or Mark Twain as they and the erudite world also thought of him, in order to learn from him how Tom too could become a famous writer of novels and be as famous, and rich, and happy as he knew Mr. Clemens must be.

Tom knew of Mr. Clemens, he explained, that he'd owned a publishing company and personally and proudly had hand delivered $200,000 to the widow of former president Ulysses S. Grant as royalty earnings from the autobiography Grant had written and Mr. Clemens had published, that he'd had lots of money to invest in a new printing machine that probably was a humdinger, and that he was invited often to lots of dinners all over the world at which he ate free and at which he made speeches for which he actually received payment. It sounded to Tom like a very good thing. And with Huck Finn gone off west for a new life in the territory, he had not much else to think about.

He had no doubt Mr. Clemens would be tickled to see him—why would he not be?—as he blithely set out from Hannibal, Missouri, to call on Mr. Clemens at his home in Hartford, Connecticut. Although he could not know it from the beginning, it was the first leg of a literary tour of discovery that would take him west to California, back east through Chicago to New York City, then all the way across the ocean into England, and back again to New York and into Massachusetts, and finally back home again with enormous relief to Aunt Polly's house in Hannibal, Missouri.

How Tom managed to travel so far and get from place to place with one change of shirt and underwear in his small bag and but few dollars in his pocket is another story (wrote Pota), so we won't go into it here, except (as Pota elected to add) that he sold his Tom Sawyer bamboo fishing pole, on which he had already carved out his name, and one autographed copy of his book, Mark Twain's *The Adventures of*

Tom Sawyer, to a collector he met on the train, signed on the spot in his own hand.

It took a while for young Tom Sawyer to find his way from the small town along the Mississippi River to the colossal showplace of a house in Hartford, Connecticut, in which he'd been told Samuel Clemens lived, and he received disappointing news when he arrived. The object of his search was not around to talk with him and probably would not have gone to the trouble to see him if he had been. Mr. Clemens was away on another of his endless speaking tours, lecturing again to earn money to continue living in his splendid house and to repay what debts he still owed from his losing ventures with a publishing business and the manufacture of a Paige typesetting machine that had not worked out as he'd hoped. Tom learned all this and more from a Mr. Rogers, who, by chance, was on the premises when Tom appeared. Mr. Rogers was a big executive of the Standard Oil trust of Mr. John D. Rockefeller's and a friend of Mr. Clemens who had taken on voluntarily the difficult responsibility of straightening out Mark Twain's mismanaged finances. When home these days, Clemens hardly saw anybody and did not receive uninvited visitors. He doubted Tom Sawyer would be an exception.

"Your Mark Twain," said Mr. Rogers, "is not the funny fellow he's supposed to be." When home, he was most often depressed over several things: over the failure of his publishing business, the failure of his typesetting machine business and the huge losses of money he had suffered, the early death of a son as a small child, for which he still blamed himself, the more recent death of a daughter while he was abroad on another speaking tour, for which he also blamed himself, the medical opinion that another of his daughters—he'd had three—was susceptible to fits of epilepsy, the poor health of his wife, and the fact that his later written works, like *The Man That Corrupted Hadleyburg* and *Pudd'nhead Wilson*, which reflected a sour, contemptuous view of civilized humanity, had not ingratiated him as widely with the public as he had been much earlier with such humorous successes as *Tom Sawyer* and *Huckleberry Finn*. "And he's not so funny anymore, and he's not too smart," confided Clemens's good friend Mr. Rogers. "If you're looking for someone to teach you how to be a prosperous writer, you ought to find someone else."

"But I imagined he'd made a lot of money out of me and Huck Finn," exclaimed Tom. "Didn't he?"

"Sure, he did. But he no sooner made it then he wanted to spend it in a very showy way. He likes attention. Look at the size of this nightmare of a mansion he's been maintaining all these years, and just to keep up good appearances with his neighbors, to show he could afford it, and now he can't. That's how writers are. The more money they make, the more they believe they're going to keep on making, and the more they want to spend to make a showy appearance of how well they're doing. It's not cheap, you know, this house. More than twenty rooms, you see, twenty-eight all told, with a library and a billiard room, and six servants. No, you probably don't know. Mr. Clemens is enslaved to his creditors, not by law but by his conscience, and that's only because he chooses to be, like an idiot, a stubborn blockhead. I am one of his creditors. I am probably his best friend, and I have sworn to him that I will sue to collect unless he does the right thing and seeks the protection of the court as a bankrupt. But he won't do that yet, as any upright businessman certainly would do; he hasn't got the character and sense enough. No, he'd rather wear himself out traveling everywhere around the world giving those funny speeches of his to make enough money to pay all his creditors off. Here he's miserable and lonely, since his daughter died, living in this enormous house, and his wife is ailing too. He's up playing billiards alone every night until three in the morning. They'll be off to Europe soon, for health spas in a better climate, so you'd better forget about him. He doesn't really want to see anybody, not even me. I have the house up for sale, Tom. And he probably won't still be living here, if you ever decide to come back. Good Lord— instead of paying that two hundred thousand dollars to Grant's widow when he owed it, he should have lied about the amount and stolen the money to keep his publishing business going. Any self-respecting businessman would have done that. Grant was dead anyway and never would have known the difference. Or better still, if things looked bad and he had good business sense, he could have siphoned the money off into his pocket and only then let the business fail. But no, not him. No sense and too much pride. Would you believe it—he put his own money into developing that typesetting machine! Can you imagine? That's no way to do business. Never put your own money into anything, Tom, if you want some good advice. What we do is borrow all we can from a bank and get what else we need from trusting friends. That way, you personally can't lose even when things go bad. But not him, your amusing Mr. Mark Twain. No sir, Tom, here's good advice. Find someone else for a mentor and a guide. If you want to learn from someone how to have a happy life as a writer, get a better model. Why don't you try tracking down that famous author Jack London somewhere out in California? There's a man who's done well. Started from nothing and has earned more than a million dollars, they say. Built a model house that's quite a showplace and developed a large model farm somewhere up north in California that uses the best and latest methods for growing things. I'd be proud to shake that man's hand, even though he says he's a socialist. Yes, my boy, Jack London is the man you want to look up to to find out how to become a famous writer and enjoy the life of a man of property. Mr. Clemens is too unhappy these years, works too hard at this lecturing and everything, and is in too much trouble over money to be an inspiration to anyone."

Despite the dire financial report, Tom found it heartening to hear that Mr. Clemens had been able to amass so much money to lose, and his aspirations for a career in writing were fortified. And Jack London had prospered too. Tom was grateful for the advice he had received and promised to go west and seek out Mr. London.

The rapid advances in railroad transportation between the end of the Civil War and the turn into the new century made the journey from Hartford, Connecticut, across the country to California no more difficult and troublesome than the voyage by steamship from Boston or New York to Liverpool, England, a separate journey that Tom, although he had no hint of it yet, was ultimately destined to make.

In due time, therefore, Tom Sawyer found himself stepping off a train into a railroad station in California. With what haste he could muster, he proceeded farther north past San Francisco to find Jack London and acquire from him what useful lessons he could toward becoming a writer of fictions as successful as Mr. Clemens or Mr. London, two of the most applauded American authors in the history of the country. Fast though Tom sped, he arrived too late.

Jack London had gone off in illness to Hawaii.

Tom naturally was disappointed to hear this. He heaved a disheartened, frustrated sigh when told. He sorely regretted he would have no opportunity to discuss his prospects with the renowned, vigorous Darwinian socialist and the self-taught philosophical adherent of Herbert Spencer, Marx, and Darwin. The author of *The Call of the Wild*, *White Fang*, the personal, autobiographical *John Barleycorn*, about his lifelong troubles with alcohol, and many, many more novels, nonfiction books, and sociological tracts than Tom knew about, or wished to, had sailed away to Hawaii in naive faith the gentler climate of the Pacific islands would mend the incurable and fatal kidney disease he'd been told was afflicting him, a malady that would lead to his death back in California but a few years later.

By suicide, the rumor insisted, Tom was later horrified to hear. The doctor recorded it officially as "a gastrointestinal urinary failure." Others, who seemed no more definitely in possession of the undivided facts, hinted at an overdose of morphine, perhaps incurred unwittingly in administering the opiate prescribed medicinally for relief from the painful anguishes of his kidney condition, perhaps done intentionally in fatigue and despair, and in fear of the imminent onslaught of poverty that threatened. His magnificent showplace of a mansion had burned, his ambitious state-of-the-agrarian-art farm of fifteen hundred acres had suffered a massive crop failure because of an early frost. He was in extreme financial difficulty. He was more and more a drunkard, it was said of him, indulging himself randomly in alcohol as had been true of him all his life. Starting from scratch as an orphan almost entirely on his own, Jack London had labored at just about everything and through writing had amassed a small fortune, earning more than a million dollars in royalties in the course of achieving his worldwide fame and traveling everywhere on all kinds of assignments and adventures. But at the end he left no wealth: London died poor, if not poor as a church mouse, then as poor as Mr. Samuel Clemens, though perhaps not yet as deeply in debt.

He was only forty.

By then, of course, Tom had long since started back down south to San Francisco with the plan of finding and conversing with Bret Harte, another American author internationally appreciated, and perhaps learning from him what it was like to live as a celebrated writer and what steps to take to become one. He was eager to find out from him as well something of his friendship and early association with Samuel Clemens, of which Tom Sawyer knew only that Harte, already an editor and perhaps the best-known author of fiction the country had then produced, had helped Clemens in the development of his first vernacular fictions (but helped him not enough, Tom as an adult was eventually forced to conclude). Tom had no doubt that the mere mention of the name Tom Sawyer to Bret Harte would be sufficient entry to Mr. Harte, and that Bret Harte would be elated to meet the popular character from the novel by Mark Twain that his own work and tutelage had helped originate.

Alas, again his timing was bad; he was again too late.

In San Francisco people in the offices of the *Overland Monthly* were astonished when Tom Sawyer showed up to introduce himself by name and announce his mission. The literary magazine was the one at which Bret Harte had distinguished himself as its first editor and as the author of those illustrious examples of the new realism in west coast fiction "The Luck of Roaring Camp" and "The Outcasts of Poker Flat." A few of the old-timers there guffawed openly as Tom ingenuously queried them about Harte. Harte, Tom was informed, had abandoned San Francisco a long time earlier for a better-paying editorial job in Chicago with the *Lakeside Monthly*, a new literary journal whose founders promised him a share of ownership too. In abandoning San Francisco, he had also abandoned a mob of furious creditors with bills owed that he had neither the means nor the stomach to pay. Harte was something of a dandy with expensive tastes and affectations.

Tom was discouraged once more, until some well-meaning person there asked why he did not try finding and talking to Ambrose Bierce. The name registered only dimly, but Tom made inquiries, learned that even Charles Dickens in England was a fan of his. Thus, Bierce assuredly seemed a person to look up.

He was in great luck, Tom thought at first, for Bierce had returned to San Francisco from England, where he had been living for something like four years. But Tom's luck quickly cooled. A sad and lonely widower was the widely esteemed author of the hallucinatory "An Occurrence at Owl Creek Bridge" and the gripping "Chickamauga," in which the deaf and dumb boy playing soldier outside his home on the Civil War battleground does not understand that the brutal war scenes raging around him are real and not merely picturesque creations of his imagination until he returns to his home and finds his mother dead, a casualty. Bierce did not want to die in bed. So, this man, who had inveighed almost all his adult life against the horrors of war, at age seventy went off into Mexico to observe the revolution of Pancho Villa against the despotic government there, and was never seen or heard of again.

Curses, thought Tom. Just my fate.

A young man of lesser makeup might have renounced his quest right then after such disillusioning experiences as he was encountering. But not Tom Sawyer. His spirits quickened—if only for the while—when he was told about the progressive realist Frank Norris and was informed that Frank Norris had a home nearby, right there in San Francisco. Great luck! thought Tom. Frank Norris, the eminent proponent of the new realism in muckraking fiction with such esteemed novels to his credit as *McTeague, The Pit*, and *The Octopus*, enjoyed a stable marriage and home life and was at the height of his flourishing literary career—and, Tom found out, was dead of appendicitis at the age of thirty-two.

Tom now had nowhere to turn but back, back east. He went by way of Chicago in hopes of catching up with Bret Harte there and learning from him what he could about writing, and about his friendship with Mark Twain.

But people in Chicago were equally astonished when Tom identified himself and announced his purpose in the office of the *Lakeside Monthly*, the periodical for which Bret Harte had left San Francisco for higher pay and to elude his creditors in California. A few of the old-timers there guffawed openly too as they listened to Tom, or covered smiles while laughing up their sleeves. They disclosed to Tom that Harte, surprisingly, had not stopped in Chicago long enough to claim the editor's job for which he had been hired. He had not appeared at the very grand and broadly publicized banquet arranged in his honor to exalt his assumption of the helm of the literary magazine. Instead, he had gone on with his wife to Boston and then New York City, and in New York City he was soon collaborating on a Broadway play with Samuel Clemens, who, they stressed, though certain Tom knew, was the name of the real human being behind the renowned pseudonym Mark Twain. And then there came a real twist to that comedy of Bret Harte, an ironic epilogue that roused more laughter. As a generous surprise to Harte, his new employers had made out a check to him for $14,000, to give as a present, a sort of signing bonus with which to welcome him to the publication and demonstrate the great extent of their appreciation. Fourteen thousand dollars in found money was a large amount, especially back then. Since Harte had not appeared at the banquet, the gift was never made, and he traveled away virtually destitute.

Neither Harte nor Mr. Clemens could be found in New York City when Tom finally arrived there. Mr. Clemens, who had since given up his large house in Hartford, Connecticut, had lived with his family in Europe awhile and then settled on Fifth Avenue in New York City. In order to pay off the last of his creditors, he was away lecturing for money again, an activity, he had stated more than once to his agent, of which he now frequently was weary and had grown often to detest. Bret Harte had lectured for money too, an activity he detested even more angrily, for he felt for his audiences a genuine contempt; Mr. Clemens at least enjoyed very much being enjoyable. And Mr. Harte, in the interim, had moved on to Europe, leaving behind a wife he never again wanted anything to do with, and his children too. Harte went first to Germany in a government position with responsibilities he neglected shamelessly and then to a government position in

Glasgow, from which office he spent so much time away in literary London among the greats, who thought more highly of his later work than did his fellow Americans, that he was eventually dismissed because of his inattention to the requirements of his job. Harte settled in London, and was soon living scandalously with, and on the generosity of, a wealthy Belgian widow, the mother of nine children. The play on which he and Clemens had worked was also gone from the city. The optimistic endeavor at collaboration had not proved a triumph. Probably, the strain of working together had contributed to the outspoken loathing Mr. Clemens had for Mr. Harte from then on, a disaffection that led him to say bluntly of Mr. Harte, when queried about him by the genteel Henry James, that he was "a son of a bitch."

Henry James was living in England, Tom learned. So was Bret Harte. And even brilliant young Stephen Crane, known throughout the western world for *The Red Badge of Courage* and *Maggie: A Girl of the Streets,* had moved to England also. Crane was especially exciting to Tom, for he was not much older. They were practically contemporaries, Tom figured. And Tom was quick to picture in that famous author a felicitous potential role model. Tom Sawyer figured he could do no better than confer with that American literary friend of Joseph Conrad's and Henry James's, young Stephen Crane, if he wished to learn anything from a novelist of prominence who was still regarded with importance and was without excruciating regrets.

And since so many American men of literature had seemed to find it easy to journey back and forth between America and England, Tom calculated correctly that he could make his way there too.

Selling autographed copies of his book was easier than writing it.

But Crane was no longer in England when Tom finally disembarked from the steamship in Liverpool and succeeded finally in making his way to London. Crane, Tom learned, had moved to England from New York with tuberculosis and a burden of debts from advances from publishers for works he had not been able to complete. He also had gone there to escape the social opprobrium arising from his having taken up with a jolly live-in companion who earlier had run a brothel in New Orleans and to end the constant harassment by New York City police officers for his having defended publicly in print an innocent victim of their abuse. More seriously ill with tuberculosis than when he had come, he had departed England for treatment in a sanatorium in Germany, and even while Tom was vacillating over whether or not to try to follow and find him, Tom Sawyer received word that Stephen Crane had died there.

The harassed young man was only twenty-eight.

Tom was stricken with grief by the news.

And Bret Harte, Tom soon learned, had already died in agony from throat cancer.

Too late again, thought Tom, bewailing his luck.

There was still Henry James.

But Henry James, hardly ever in the best of health, was in another one of his deep depressions and categorically refused to see him or anyone new. Among the factors contributing to his temper of heavy despair were the recent death of his brother William; a family history of emotional disorders; a declining position in the world of literature; the successive, accumulating failures in popularity of his latest, deepest, largest, greatest novels, *The Wings of the Dove, The Ambassadors, The Golden Bowl,* which had each been received with little praise, much belittlement, and small readership; the something like four years of concentrated labor for a New York edition of his collected works that had yielded results of small appeal and total royalties of less than one hundred pounds; the denigrating criticism he'd received in print from H. G. Wells and other figures of authority; and, of lesser, even trivial nature, the luxury rides in the new automobile owned by his affluent good friend Edith Wharton, whose thinner, simpler, easily accessible novels were proving far more likable with the reading public and bringing her more honor and income than he could win for his. Plus the nearly insufferable indignity of discovering that she had secretly been taking up a collection for him!

No, there was no chance at all Henry James would talk to Tom Sawyer, the retainer in the Chelsea apartment curtly reported. If there was anything he hoped to learn from Mr. James, Tom Sawyer might read all he'd written, if he could bring himself to do that. Or as perhaps an easier alternative, he could speak with the acquaintance and distinguished literary admirer of Mr. James, the novelist Joseph Conrad.

Tom had of course heard that name Joseph Conrad and was galvanized by the chance to speak to the famous novelist of Polish descent who had written in English. Making what haste he could to track down the whereabouts of Mr. Conrad, he proceeded directly to his home in Kent, not far from where Mr. James had his own country home in the town of Rye, to call on him. But as expeditiously as he traveled, he was again too late.

Joseph Conrad was in the throes of a severe nervous breakdown and unwilling to speak to anyone about anything, and unable to speak in anything but Polish. So devastating was his mental collapse that he had forgotten completely his knowledge of English. As with Henry James, poor Joseph Conrad's most recent novels, novels like *Lord Jim*, *Nostromo*, and *Under Western Eyes* that are now universally numbered among his best, had not fared well and had brought a downfall in what reputation and small earning power he'd enjoyed. Furthermore, a revolution in literary taste of a kind that unfortunately repeatedly appears in the world of letters to erode the stature of established figures was shifting away in a direction not advantageous to him. And to top all that off, he'd been faced with an urgent, growing, unsatisfied need for money: letters of desperation to his publishers were yielding little; they'd grown increasingly deaf and less responsive to his pleas for amounts due him or for advances on future works. Conrad often rued the day, only in Polish, for the time being, that he had embarked on a career so harshly unaccommodating as the writing of novels. Having long before earned his papers as a sea captain, he had tried without result to secure a berth on a ship in order to go back to sea and the healthier enjoyment of a much simpler and much better life than he was stomaching in literature.

Good gosh, Tom wondered, with the chilling alarm of a disagreeable insight, was none of them but Edith Wharton able to earn enough to live on in peace and continue performing the work she wanted to? But poor Wharton, to her misfortune, had married a wastrel, a drunkard who'd plundered her inheritance, and endured a woeful marriage.

And now poor Tom could think of nothing next to do on this literary pilgrimage of his but sail back.

Aboard ship coming home, finding not much else to divert him during the endless hours and days of the ocean voyage, he, despite the knowledge of biographical calamities he was gathering, nonetheless grasped at what seemed a smashing idea and engaged himself in an enterprise multitudes of adults before and since have elected to busy themselves with for recreation when they could find nothing more entertaining to do: Tom Sawyer thought of writing a novel!

And the more he thought of it, the more sensible the idea seemed to him. He'd been reading so many poor novels of late (including a couple by Mr. Clemens himself) that he had to feel he could not do worse. A Tom Sawyer novel, by Tom Sawyer himself, perhaps with Mark Twain as coauthor, the newest in a continuation of the series of books about him that Mr. Clemens had already launched long before under his world-famous pen name. Tom had no doubt such a book would sell many copies, or that the idea would now be pleasing to Mr. Clemens, who might jump at this chance to make some easy money and indeed suggest collaborating with him. *Tom Sawyer Abroad* had already been used, but maybe *Tom Sawyer Abroad by Tom Sawyer Himself* could now be done and was a good idea, or *Tom Sawyer, Traveler*—that one sounded good to him too.

Once cleared through customs and immigration, Tom hurried with his notes and outline to Mr. Twain's newest dwelling, which now was a house in Redding, Connecticut.

There he was presented with more tragic news. Mr. Clemens had returned not long before from a stay in Florence, Italy, where he had gone with his wife, Olivia, both now in poor health, both suffering the aches of rheumatism, both seeking a more agreeable climate to ameliorate the miseries of their ailments. And there, Olivia had weakened and died.

In Redding, a widower, he had set up residence with his daughter Clara, the one susceptible to epileptic seizures. And in Redding she too had died shortly before, suffering a seizure in a bathtub and drowning there. Mr. Clemens did not wish to speak with him. Three of his four children had died before he did, and his wife too had died. When living in New York City, he'd dashingly worn glaring white suits strolling the avenues because he wished to attract attention and be recognized.

Tom was not feebleminded and charitably understood and forgave the reluctance of Mr. Clemens to receive him. The thought did not once cross his innocent mind that Samuel Clemens, who'd authored *The Adventures of Tom Sawyer, Tom Sawyer, Detective*, and *Tom Sawyer Abroad*, had come to *loathe* that very name Tom Sawyer, as he now bitterly did very much else in the world around him.

Tom was adrift now in his literary expedition, and his zeal for a career as an author had understandably lessened considerably. Since he was already in Connecticut, he allowed curiosity alone to carry him farther north into New England to Concord, Massachusetts, to find out what he could about still another American literary idol. He believed that Nathaniel Hawthorne had died there many years before. He had not known, however, that Mr. Hawthorne too, always a solitary and somber person, had struggled all his life to earn enough from his serious writing to sustain himself and his family while continuing to work at what he wished to, had fallen out of favor with the public and publishers, and had lived his last years in wretched solitude and with declining creative powers, suffering psychotic deteriorations that found their way incoherently into his last, persistent, unpublished writings.

Coming back through Boston, Tom found out that late in life Henry Wadsworth Longfellow, a college classmate of Hawthorne's at Bowdoin College and at one time a Harvard professor and the country's most celebrated poet, had endured moods of extreme melancholy after the death of his wife, in a fire at home, before his very eyes, and the inescapable perception that other poets, like Walt Whitman and Edgar Allan Poe, had shown not the slightest liking for the rhymed metrical versification that had been the talent endearing him so long to so many average readers.

Sad, thought Tom, commiserating with the unfortunate old man, very sad.

Intrigued by the new favorite, Emily Dickinson, he set off for Amherst, Massachusetts, which was not that distant from Boston. There, he was astounded to learn that Emily Dickinson, a determined recluse who'd never married, had been dead more than twenty years and that all of the more than fifteen hundred poems now finding large favor with a critical audience had been published posthumously and had not even been submitted by her for acceptance. Very much earlier she had suffered patronizing comments and rejection. A queer woman indeed, she had just about totally secluded herself in her home for more than fifteen years, writing more or less in secrecy, seeing almost no one, scarcely venturing into the home of her brother and his wife, which was next door to her own. Queer, thought Tom, and a lamentable shame she had not enjoyed in her lifetime the sweet triumphs and vindication of her brilliant, provocative talents. She wore white always and, though subject to spells of swooning that had caused her to fall down her staircase more than once, the iso-

lated, eccentric poetic genius would not allow a doctor into
her room to examine her.

Back in New York, Tom now found there was hardly anybody famous left to talk to about a life in writing. He discovered with dismay that the esteemed poet, literary reviewer,
and short story author Edgar Allan Poe, penniless, alcoholic,
paranoid, perhaps drug addicted, had fallen into a drunken
delirium in a street in Baltimore, clothed in disreputable gar-
ments possibly not his own, and had died in a hospital there
three days later. No one could ever figure out how he had got
there, what he was doing there. Poe, disoriented and unintel-
ligible, could not help.

Tom next thought of Hawthorne's friend Herman Melville
and wondered if it might prove possible to track him down if
he was still alive and in New York City. He soon learned that
Melville was not alive. And had he still been living there, Tom
would not have been able to find him, for Melville had spent
his last years in poverty and obscurity, without a public and
without a publisher. As with others whose best novels had
brought demoralizing failure and a decline in reputation,
Melville's final best efforts led to the ruination of his career as
a writer and to his despair as a man. There were times his
wife and in-laws were convinced he had gone insane. His fan-
tastic earlier symbolist story "Bartleby the Scrivener," Mr.
William Dean Howells had clarified for Tom, could easily be
read as an autobiographical protest of a man, or any author,
unwilling to go back to merely repeating, to copying, his popular romantic novels of the South Seas when consumed by
such literary visions as *Moby-Dick* and *Pierre; or, The Ambigui-
ties* and his extraordinary modernist work *The Confidence*

Man, impressive accomplishments each that had cost him his public and cost him his publishers. Not until thirty years after his death was his haunting and perplexing *Billy Budd* published. Melville, like Clemens and Harte, had gone out lecturing for money too.

Tom learned much of this in Boston from the notable magazine editor Mr. William Dean Howells, a close friend of Mr. Clemens who had known personally almost all the writers encountered, or missed, in Tom Sawyer's fruitless pilgrimage. Tom could have indeed found out much more from Mr. Howells, whose own meteoric appearance as a distinguished novelist at the turn of the century had slimmed into his distinguished career as editor of the *Atlantic Monthly*. But Tom had by now lost all interest in his subject; he was in fact shamed and repelled by the nauseating memory of his former passion.

His literary ambition had waned, his curiosity was sated with discoveries about the lives of literary celebrities that were cumulatively appalling. His travels through the literary hall of fame of America had steered him into a mortuary of a museum with the failed lives and careers of suffering heroes who were only human. These were not the heroes of the ancient Greeks and Trojans like Achilles, Hector, Zeus, and Hera. These were only driven human beings of high intentions who wished to be writers and who, in most other respects, seemed more than normally touchy, neurotic, mixed up, and unhappy.

Abruptly, Tom Sawyer wanted only to go home. He had seen enough, he felt, of the literary life. To a collector in New York he peddled another autographed copy of his book, the last he owned, and with the money obtained he sped back in luxury to his house in Missouri.

. . .

"Tom?"

"Hello, Aunt Polly, hello, Aunt Polly, I'm home, I'm home!" Tom hailed her in good cheer from the downstairs landing.

Oh, shit, thought Aunt Polly. He's back. Now I won't be able to go about all day in my housecoat, will I? I hope he's given up that lunatic idea of becoming a writer. I think I'll go mad if I have to sit in a chair and listen to him read to me. Oh, Lord, do I deserve that?

She was quickly reassured.

Tom Sawyer would no sooner think of a career writing fiction for a living then placing himself in front of an oncoming locomotive or diving headlong from the highest cliff he could find into the Mississippi River. No, he was aglow with a better aim. He would train to become a pilot on a Mississippi steamboat, as Mr. Clemens had done for some four years and could convincingly look back on as the happiest time of his life.

Tom quickly found out he was too late for that one too.

After the Civil War, railroads had totally destroyed commercial steamboat traffic on the Mississippi and there were no jobs as pilots to be had.

Ever enterprising, he in minutes hit upon an idea equally sound.

He would train to become a railroad engineer and guide his locomotive freely about wherever the railroad tracks led.

And if that proved too difficult to learn, he would go east to a college for a business course and study how to be a capitalist and become a millionaire.

There were now so many of them, it had to be easy.

My talk this evening is about writers and writing (began Eugene Pota in an auditorium at the university in South Carolina, to which he had gone, when invited, to lecture, like Clemens, Harte, and Melville much earlier on, for a fee, of course; with Pota, the money was not the principal factor, but, with Pota as always, it *was* a factor). It's a talk about a life in literature and—you might be surprised to hear—is cheerily called . . . "The Literature of Despair." (He was speaking genially from an outline of notes, while trying with composure to recall the sentences and sequence he had for a week or two been rehearsing in his head.)

The title is not, as you may think, a reference to the tormented and despairing people in familiar novels, characters like Jay Gatsby, Lord Jim, Gregor Samsa, or Joseph K; to Bartleby the Scrivener or Captain Ahab, Madame Bovary, Anna Karenina, or Alyosha Karamazov—or *any* in that amazing, hyperactive family of Karamazovs. (Here, Pota paused with a look of mild surprise, as though the trailing remark was a spontaneous afterthought, which indeed it had been, and waited for the low chuckle to come in response and recognition. It did.) Instead, my title refers to literary works *about* the authors who wrote such novels and what an examination of the lives of these authors reveals.

The idea came to me shortly after reading in a fairly concentrated time a number of books, or reviews of books, that were newly published biographies of some very famous authors, one of F. Scott Fitzgerald, another of Charles Dickens, and another of Henry James. They came out together, so to speak, and I was struck all at once by the tragic component that was present in the life of each of them, especially in their late years.

I had already known about Dickens from previous biographers, and of course, I'd known about Fitzgerald and his excessive drinking. But Henry James, I confess, was new to me. That this man, exercising always such a knowledgeable air of authority and intellectual self-discipline and restraint—a man who, in that matchless description of T. S. Eliot's, "had a mind so fine that no idea could violate it" (Now, thought Pota as his audience responded, just what the hell *does* that mean— they seem to know, but I still don't)—should be vulnerable to psychosomatic ailments and spells of depression late in life, came as a shock.

Three authors, three unhappy men.

Another surprise was Joseph Conrad, when I learned a bit later on, again from a biography, of his difficulties earning money and of his severe nervous breakdown late in life.

John Cheever's diaries were published, posthumously, in that same period, and they are as sad, so sad, a personal testament as anyone would ever wish to read.

Let me give you now a hasty roll call of some other well-known writers to whom that word *despair* might be applied, at least to part of their lives and their careers.

In the last century there was—and here I am consulting a vertical list of names—to begin with:

Edgar Allan Poe, alcoholic and mentally disturbed. Nathaniel Hawthorne and Herman Melville too, with their need for money and their failing careers and resulting periods of depression.

Turning from that century into this one, let us see how much the life in literature has improved for those practicing it, right up into our own times. We have Henry James, as I've already said, and in Washington, D.C., Henry Adams, with what might then, in a man, be diagnosed as neurasthenia, and in a woman, less flatteringly, be called "the vapors." Today we know it as . . . depression.

Joseph Conrad as a youth tried at least once to kill himself; he shot himself in the chest, aiming for his heart, but missed (a pause, Pota decided, for some uncomfortable laughter).

Jack London, that best-selling author, was all his life a very heavy drinker, and wrote at least one novel about it. Of more recent vintage, so was Malcolm Lowry, whose excellent novel *Under the Volcano*, about an unregenerate alcoholic, also was written in a mode of autobiography.

In America into our own time, among the very heavy drinkers often disabling themselves we have—I am going down a list I have here (Didn't I just say something like that? he wondered, reproaching himself):

Eugene O'Neill.

Edmund Wilson.

Sinclair Lewis, our first Nobel Prize winner for literature, who drank so heavily that H. L. Mencken—no teetotaler he—could not bear to be with him.

William Faulkner, long and widely noted for his drunkenness, who died from injuries after a drunken fall from a horse.

Theodore Dreiser, another novelist about whose heavy drinking Mencken commented.

And as I've already said, F. Scott Fitzgerald.

And back in England, let's see who else we have:

Evelyn Waugh, right off, notoriously alcoholic, and notoriously bad natured and rude.

Kingsley Amis, a drinker of spirits, died after a fall down a staircase, possibly after drinking—I've come that close to falling down staircases myself after a martini or two.

And in England again, as I believe I've just said, there was Malcolm Lowry, not only habitually drunk but also another probable suicide, from an overdose of medications that most thought deliberate.

The same was and is still suspected of Jack London, by the way—that he did kill himself, at the age of forty.

And back to the British, perhaps a regiment of others I don't know about or have forgotten—Graham Greene now comes to mind, and then, of course, Dylan Thomas, who collapsed from drink in New York and died there, before the age of forty, and Brendan Behan, Irish rather than British but no less the drinking man.

And James Joyce, if I remember correctly, was a heavy wine drinker with a falling-down-drunk-in-the-street capacity.

Truman Capote fits into this category, probably, both for his excessive drinking later on and for what we may call his sedative medications.

Tennessee Williams also fits in, with his drinking and pill

popping. He choked to death on the cap of a bottle of pills he was trying to take. People do not commit suicide that way; but sober people do not often die that way either.

Ernest Hemingway, also for a long time a very serious drinker, eventually, as we all know, deteriorated into paranoid depression and committed suicide. John O'Hara, a very heavy drinker, as was John Steinbeck—heavier and heavier, I suspect, as working grew more difficult and their reputations declined.

Apart from drinking, odd, untypical behavior also exists. J. D. Salinger moved from New York City and withdrew from normal social life as a genuine and resolute recluse. Thomas Pynchon, despite the prizes won for his novels, has never allowed himself into the public eye, not even to be photographed.

Unhappy successful novelists who felt like failures? William Gaddis, who twice won important literary prizes for two separate novels, each time felt slighted by the two separate publishers immediately afterward, who ignored him, he felt.

Next I have on my list other writers who are, or were, my contemporaries—Jerzy Kosinsky and Richard Brautigan, both suicides.

Before your time—for most of you young ones here, I think—Ross Lockridge, the author of a huge success of a best-selling novel, *Raintree County*, and Thomas Heggen, author of the novel and the hit play *Mister Roberts*, were both suicides.

Now, just what was it that made death preferable to the lives they were living? To tell you the honest truth: I don't know. And I don't want to guess.

Among women, Emily Dickinson was strangely, neurotically reclusive; Virginia Woolf drowned herself—walked into a river with weights in her pockets. Anne Sexton and Sylvia Plath, each a suicide—but if I wanted to extend my list into poets, I don't know where I would be able to stop. Hart Crane, age thirty-three, threw himself off a passenger ship to kill himself. Randall Jarrell is the one I believe to be the depressed poet who many thought walked deliberately out into the road in front of an oncoming automobile—or maybe it was some other poet—maybe both. Robert Lowell, hospitalized more than once for alcoholism and violent manic behavior. Delmore Schwartz, editor, poet, short story writer, considered by many contemporaries to be among the brightest literary lights of his time, went violently insane and died in a mental institution. John Berryman, the poet at the height of his career, I believe surprised everyone by throwing himself off a building or a bridge. James Dickey consciously or not did all he could to drink himself to death: it took time, but he persisted, and in time succeeded.

Now, once off on this train of thought, it was not hard to keep going. Among my contemporaries, more than one has spoken frankly of personal encounters with depression serious enough to require professional treatment (Haven't I already said this and mentioned the names? Pota asked himself without faltering), so it would be—so it is revealing no secrets to mention their names, but I'd rather not. (If I ever do this one again, Pota decided, shuffling papers to allow himself a pause, I'd rather write it all out fully, and *then* ad-lib.) Among them, though, is Art Buchwald, the *lifelong* humorist, the humorist to this day, who is able to find fun in just about anything.

And Mario Puzo had said more than once in public interviews that he owed the last several years of his life, and his most recent novel, to the ameliorating effects of Prozac.

Now all these I've mentioned are successful writers of some reputation—successful at least as writers.

One has to tremble at the thought of the emotional state, the casualty rate, among writers who have been moderately successful, or not successful at all, of the very, very many who published one novel or two to good reviews, and then melted out of recognition into other occupations and have hardly ever been heard of again.

What, then, are the reasons, I have to wonder, that make the biographical information of so many of them a body of literature of despair?

And the answer I give again, is that I don't know. And neither, I feel, does anybody else.

Now, I'm aware that the information I've supplied and the conclusions I've implied are not statistically sound.

For one thing, there is no control group to measure this frequency of psychological disorder against the general population. It could be that right here, within this audience listening to me tonight, there are a great many of us who are drunk, depressed, and on the very verge of committing suicide. (Pota lightly joined in the tittering.)

For another, there are other writers of large and not so large reputation who breeze through life, as far as we know, with hardly an unusual, agitated ruffle.

Nevertheless, I find it just about impossible to think of another occupational group with the same incidence of severe unhappiness and distress among the most famed and accomplished figures.

It is almost enough to chill the heart of the parent whose

child declares the wish to seek a career as an author! You must spring right into action to save that child. Stop it—if you can. Nip that ambition in the bud. Guide that child instead into beating drums, or a career as a juggler.

Fitzgerald, in an obituary of his good friend Ring Lardner, writes that Lardner . . . had stopped finding fun in his work ten years before he died. Lardner, another humorist, had also been a very heavy drinker, an alcoholic. And of the occupation of writing, Fitzgerald notes, and I emphasize, *"within the practice of your trade you were forever . . . unsatisfied."*

Kurt Vonnegut, as I think I've said (Have I or have I not? Pota questioned himself), has hinted in his written work at his own encounters with depression, and he has vowed publicly that he would attempt no more books. To those who know him, he thus far seems much relieved by that decision—liberated, so to speak, and I can almost understand . . . and (Pota lifted his eyes, affecting a dreamy expression) almost envy him. William Styron wrote his well-known and widely read work on depression, *Darkness Visible*. However, Styron and Vonnegut are still around and functioning actively, and *so* am I.

But I do think that the three of us could easily understand and echo the dolorous sentiments I've been quoting . . . and am about to.

There are factors in the life of creative writing that stem, I believe, from, *one*, something in the nature of the occupation itself; *two*, something unhappy in the early experience of the person that antedates the occupation; *three*, a tendency in early childhood for dreaming extravagant wishes for a much richer life than one is experiencing; *four*, a wish to be—most important, I'd say—a wish to be outstanding, to excel at almost *anything* that will excite admiration from family and friends and the society at large, and writing for them offers a promising outlet; and, *four*—did I just do number four?—anyway, *four*, most probably, a combination of some, or *all*.

F. Scott Fitzgerald is a good example. From childhood through adolescence through college, Fitzgerald did long to perform . . . to stand out . . . as a football star . . . a writer . . . a stage performer . . . at just about anything.

And at the tender age of twenty-four he was a celebrated American novelist, with a new marriage to a young Southern girl, and just a little while after that, he was standing out also as a famous drunkard, a vigorous, uninhibited alcoholic, as an embarrassing cutup and a severe trial to his friends.

Or consider young William Faulkner, before he was an author, returning from Canada after World War I, with an English walking stick and a Royal Canadian Air Force uniform he had himself ordered tailored, returning with tall, untrue stories of aviation exploits and putting on airs that earned him from neighbors the homespun, apt nickname "Count No Account."

Now, certainly we know multitudes of moody, brooding, daydreaming, contemplative young people who never give much thought to writing. So, one essential thing more: a talent, a gift, perhaps a compulsion, a propensity for sifting experiences into fantasized new events and situations and for putting them down onto paper. The talent itself is not so much the cause of anything that follows in later life, I believe, as it is perhaps a blessed outlet for discontents that already exist—a blessed outlet, at least for the while.

And then, alas, there are indeed factors in the life of the writer itself that almost inevitably lead to feelings of defeat, disappointment, frustration . . . of being unsatisfied.

To begin with, there is the work itself: the doubts about the ability to continue. The modern successful author is never entirely secure in his position and never totally at ease not knowing that he will be judged as good in the future as he has been in the past.

Next, with literary success, there also seem to come a number of realities that contribute considerably to the biographies of so many authors that I have called a literature of despair.

What happens?

First, what happens just about inevitably is that early success leads invariably to greater, grandiose expectations and also, sooner or later, to lesser success, to decreased popularity, to more exacting scrutiny and exacting criticism—to which none of us is insensitive—and to feelings of failure, even when the new accomplishments are recognized.

After all, a new talent can be discovered only once, a new star can burst upon the scene only one time.

Next, money—a diminished income. Even when the income is large, it is bound to be less than what we dreamed it would be, and less than we have become accustomed to enjoy. It is wryly amusing for the moment, for just one moment, to perceive how often the letters of authors are pleas for money that is needed, or wanted, desperately—from Fitzgerald for loans from his literary agent or publisher, from James Joyce, Conrad, even Hemingway to finance another divorce—and from Charles Dickens, demands.

And next, *three,* thirdly, I think, if I'm counting right, there looms the fear of an exhaustion of talent. There is, or should be, an unwillingness among most of us to tell the same tale twice, and a morbid feeling of deficiency when we feel we are doing that.

And, *four*—again four? (There was congenial laughter, and he again joined in.) And finally, inevitably, there is that process of aging itself, of slowing down, of weakened ambition and mental energy, especially since the early ambition has largely been realized. But age, and that depression that often comes with it, does not apply to several I've mentioned, whose lives came to an end relatively young.

And finally, finally again, I think, I would surmise at a Freudian disappointment: what did they—we—hope to obtain when they—we—first hoped to succeed as a writer?

Whatever it was, they—we—didn't get it all, and the good effects did not last. The ancient wishes were not entirely fulfilled by literary success; whatever pain or doubt or loneliness they—we—suffered was not eradicated; the status and self-esteem they—we—hoped to establish for a lifetime did not suffice for a lifetime.

And as is apt to happen to all of us, the feeling recurs that we are, in our character and personality, right back where we begin; we are the same person after all, older, wiser, but unchanged otherwise, equally needy, equally vulnerable.

Fitzgerald must have been elated at the good reviews his *Great Gatsby* received, and brokenhearted by the poor sales.

Hemingway must have been thrilled by the enormous public success of his *For Whom the Bell Tolls,* and wounded by the disparaging criticism.

And also, suddenly, there are new works appearing by new writers, and the attention of the critics and the critical public shifts. The spotlight is elsewhere. We are no longer main attractions, and that melancholy feeling creeps in that we are just about right back where we began, and much the same person after all. Just older.

F. Scott Fitzgerald is quoted, sadly, somewhere to the effect that, after a last brief meeting with Ernest Hemingway at an occasion in which Hemingway was the star and he was all but ignored, Hemingway could now speak with all the authority of success, while he, Fitzgerald, could speak with the authority of failure.

He could not foresee, nor could anyone, that Hemingway, with all the authority of success, was fated to decline into severe depression and ultimately end his life in an untidy manner, with a shotgun burst to the head.

By coincidence, even as I was preparing this talk, I found the following in an excellent work by that excellent author John Barth, *On with the Story:* his narrator, a university professor giving courses in creative writing, says, "I advise my students to read biographies of the great writers they admire—but I recommend they skip the final chapters . . . skip the endings . . . the biographical endings."

Why? For the reasons I think I've already given. More often than not, they are likely to end unhappily . . . in a literature of despair.

And now, next—among the first of the questions you're going to ask me when I've finished is this one: What about me?

And the answer I give you is: No, not yet. Thank God.

And because of all of you here tonight, not for a good while yet—not as long as there are people like you still interested in hearing me speak and eager to ask me questions about my work and other things.

So, thanks still again. And now for the rest of your questions.

Among the two questions he later recalled with good humor was this one:

"Mr. Pota, you've been writing a long time and have experience with different kinds of problems. I've been writing, or trying to write, a shorter time and wonder how you deal with this problem. What do you do when you have what's been called a writer's block?"

Pota replied without hesitating. "I've never had one."

And this one too:

"There's always much sex in your novels, and your male characters think and talk about it a lot. Do you yourself still think about sex often?"

Again Pota did not hesitate. "Every day! Hundreds of times! Without fail! Hundreds of times, every single day!"

There was laughter and much applause as he concluded with that one.

They just don't know, do they? murmured Pota to himself in a moment of twinging gloom, walking from the stage with a gesture at a lighthearted wave. They thought I was joking.

Polly was happy to have him home safely. He was relieved to be back with her. She'd been icing in the freezer a glass for his martini. The speech went well, he replied when she asked.

"They liked you?"

"Very much."

"They always do, don't they?"

"They always seem to. It's a talent I have, to make myself pleasing. It was a lively, lovely audience. It also turns out to be a pretty good talk. I might write it out coherently and try to have it published somewhere when I've got nothing better to work on. Everyone was happy, especially me. And they gave me my check."

Polly laughed, her eyes shining, her cheeks reddening, her face glistening, as always happened when she was in cheerful spirits. "They gave you the check?"

"Right there on the spot, as soon as I finished."

"I think they should always do that. I don't think it's right when they make you wait."

"And you have to count the days and wonder if it's really going to come."

"I was worried about your plane, having to land in the middle of that rainstorm."

"So was I, I was worried too," Pota told her. "But the car ride out back here was even worse. The limo driver was a right-wing bigot who wanted to tell long stories. And I had to pretend to be sleeping almost all the way out to make him shut up. Then when we left the highway he didn't know the roads, and I had to keep telling him. The fog was pretty bad."

He did not, of course, tell her about his flirtatious bantering, at the lively, large reception afterward, with two former graduate students, now poised young women in their forties, he'd first met almost fifteen years before when asked to escort them about New York to a literary gathering place on a risky weekend vacation they'd ventured to take away from their husbands. And he had not, of course, told Polly about the phone calls to the three women from the past. Both these two were divorced now and seemed gladly content with that state. They'd matured nicely, he thought, and were fashionable in appearance and well mannered and composed. Enrolled at that time in a graduate creative writing program, they'd been elated at the prospect of meeting authors and editors they'd heard about. He'd brought them both to dinner at a well-known publishing gathering place. He left one of them, the more outgoing of the two, comfortably in a group in the restaurant, where she elected to stay, and brought the other back up to his studio apartment to show her his workplace and his striking nighttime view of the Hudson River and the lighted expanse beyond.

"And you probably don't remember," she said.

"Of course I do," he cut in to protest.

"But you gave me a choice."

"I was a boor? I misbehaved? I doubt that."

"No. I wish you had been. You were the perfect gentleman. Too perfect. Kind and protective."

"That sounds more like me. It was my obligation."

"And you said you would take me right back to my hotel in a taxi if I wanted to leave, or I could spend the night or part of it right there with you."

"And you chose to leave. Of course I remember. Did you think I would forget an intrigue like that one?"

"I was scared stiff." She laughed nervously.

"I could see." He laughed too.

"I didn't know what I really wanted to do. At that time I'd never even kissed a man outside my marriage."

"You told me that, and hoped I'd understand."

"You were the first, when you kissed me good night that way in the taxi."

"I had to make a pass at you, didn't I? That was also my obligation. It would have been uncomplimentary to you if I didn't, wouldn't it? But that was not the only reason. We were having a laughing good time together, and it would have been nice. I wanted to very much. And you would have felt much worse if I hadn't, wouldn't you?"

"Yes. I was pleased you wanted to, very pleased, even though I was nervous. And you gave me a promise, a guarantee. Do you remember that part?"

"Did I? A guarantee?"

"Yes, I remember that much too. You said that if I stayed and went to bed with you then, we would have a good time and I'd probably never be sorry. But if I didn't, you could practically guarantee I would look back every time I remembered and regret I didn't. And you know something?"

"I know exactly. Or you wouldn't be saying this now."

"I have regretted it."

"Of course."

"Every time I've looked back and thought of it. I do regret it now, seeing you again and listening to you tonight. You were so good."

"Would you like another chance?" Pota was more pleased with her than he could say.

"I might." She hesitated, colored a bit, and lowered her voice so that only he could hear. "Maybe I would."

He laughed now, modestly. "It may be too late," he apologized in a likable way, intending to be unconvincing. "I might be too old now to do much, but I would sure like to try."

She was laughing too. "I don't think you'd be too old."

"Then maybe next time, whenever that might be."

After a pause in which she bit her lip, hesitating, she said, with another laugh, perhaps only half serious, "Well, let's see. Where are you staying? I could drive you back to your hotel and we can have a drink and talk a bit."

"I'm tied up with Professor Lowe and the dean," he lied on the spot, motivated and surprised by an involuntary bolt of fright. "And they're driving me to the airport right after

177

breakfast tomorrow. Maybe we could exchange addresses, on the chance I come back, or you come to New York."

She understood without words his reluctance to provide his phone or his fax number. It was unlikely he'd be back for a long time. If she ever came to New York, he vowed when alone in his hotel, he would employ whatever deceptions he had to in order to see her, then he immediately vowed he would not, no matter how strong his desire. Probably, he would back off again, as he'd just done, and make more untruthful excuses. In mock disgust, he chided himself for his initial, impulsive wish:

Pota, are you crazy? Just who do you think you are? You'll soon be seventy-six. Are you never going to grow up? Are you going to keep falling in love with just about every woman who speaks to you with some open fondness?

And he told himself yes, he certainly would. It was too late to change, and he was glad.

He loved women and always had, the idea of them, the way they dressed and looked, the smell and sound and shape of them. And there were now so many he met and saw he felt he would like to fall in love with, at least for a while, and so little time left. And given without prearrangement a conducive and fortunate setting, he automatically knew he might eagerly yield to temptation without a second thought, with some fear of discovery and the potential upset at home, but with the clearest conscience.

Even though he knew, he reminded himself, that love affairs were no longer cost effective at his age, and that he definitely did not want another divorce.

Polly seemed to sense all this anyway with an intelligent feminine intuition. She seemed animated sexually, in a good-natured way often sparked by the sight of some woman in a gathering paying too much attention to him. Pota, sitting with his arm around her and his hand under her arm, rubbed the side of her breast with his thumb. Immediately, Polly turned in against him with a warm, long kiss on the mouth. Upstairs she abandoned herself unasked to the tricks and practices of a hectic lechery she did not often display anymore since the early days when they were, as he liked to put it, still crazy about each other. She was the Dutch prostitute in the Amsterdam window again, which was a role she'd relished when they'd been in Amsterdam together, and she attempted the body massage he had detailed to her one time from his single experience in a Bangkok massage parlor. They took a long time, for neither was in a hurry. And he loved it all. He loved the extra flab of her full backside, the fine feel of the abundant female flesh wherever he touched, of her thighs, belly, and bust. He slept better by himself but always cherished the presence of a woman beside him. She surprised him with ice cubes. He was in love with her too, again.

A PAIN IN THE NECK

"It's new to me," said the doctor.

"A pain in the neck? I thought it was rather common."

"Not in my experience, it isn't. I've never seen it before, or anything like it. You had no heavy blow? Nothing hit you?"

"No," he said. "I did do a lot of twisting around in the bedroom the other night. With my wife."

"It doesn't sound venereal."

"No, it doesn't. Of course not. It hurt the next day and it's been hurting ever since."

"That shouldn't do it. No numbness in the shoulder or arms? No tingling?"

"No numbness or tingling. Just this stiffness when I try to turn my head."

"Stiffness? That's what you said?"

"Yes. A stiff neck."

"Paralysis?"

"No. It's just hard to turn it all the way, it hurts a bit when I try. I'm just surprised you haven't dealt with this before."

"Never heard of anything like it. It sounds bad, very bad. Mysterious. I think we'd better get down inside there as soon as possible and see what we can find out."

"What are you talking about?" he asked, with fearful surprise.

"I'll get you an appointment with an orthopedic surgeon—"

"No, you won't."

"—I trust who's very good at neck work."

"Surgeon? Neck work? What the hell are you talking about?"

"It's cheaper and faster in the long run to go right into surgery and get to the bottom of things as soon as you can."

"Just like that? For a stiff neck?"

"Why not? Trust me."

"Sol, do you know how they say 'Fuck you' in Hollywood?"

"How?"

"'Trust me.'"

"Thanks, Gene. I'll remember to use that one. Try to look at it my way. Why waste your time and money on a CAT scan or MRI? Something either shows up or doesn't, right? If something shows up, they'll have to go in and correct it. If nothing shows up, they'll have to go in anyway to find out what's going on. It's better my way. Let me get you an appointment."

"Don't get me any appointment yet, not with any orthopedic surgeon."

"A neurosurgeon then? Would you prefer that? If you want a second opinion, I can give you one right now by repeating what I've been saying."

"I don't want any surgeon, not yet. And I can get my own second opinion, if you don't mind. Let me just rest a few days and see if it goes away."

"Well, if you feel that's the way you want to go about it, go ahead." All of this said with a perfectly straight face. "But I think you're wasting time. Sooner or later in life you're going to have to have a surgeon. But okay. Do it your way. You might want to try some painkillers while you're waiting, aspirin or Tylenol, and a muscle relaxant like Valium, and try sleeping on a low pillow or no pillow at all."

"Thanks, Sol."

"And let me know. Let me know when you do want the surgeon. They're all very busy these days."

From Top to Bottom
(or)
From Head to Toe
(Notes)

Head:
Neck—A pain in the
Throat —A frog in the; a lump in the
Eye—A gleam in the; a poke in the
Mouth—A gift horse in the; a punch in the
Tongue—in cheek
Brain—A -----storm;
       A stroke (?)—of luck . . . (a good one)
Ear—A bug in his

Torso:
Side—A thorn in the
Chest—
Back—An aching
Heart—Burn
Liver—(?)
Kidney—A stone in the
Spine—of a book (?) (Pun?)
Bile— (Find something, for that or spleen)
Palm—An itching of the

Bottom:
Ass—A pain in the; a kick in the; a bug up the
Hip—and thigh

Balls—A kick in the; a breaker of
Cock—of the walk; a ----teaser
Knee—Water on the
Calf—A fatted (?) (Puns?) (Probably not)
Foot—in the door
Heel—A heel of Achilles
Sole—?

      Sole—bottom, foot, fish (?)
      Soul—brain, head, top

(Make something of this, something good!)

Now find a plot, or at least a plan, dammit!

THE ANATOMY LESSON

A New Novel

by

Eugene Pota

"Not bad. It's neat and it's catchy."

"Yeah, that's why I picked it. I thought so too."

"As did all of the others."

"Others?" demanded Pota. "What others?"

"All the others before you who've already used it. Do you really think you're the first author to like that as a title?"

"*The Anatomy Lesson*? For a novel?"

"Right off I can think of at least two we've done in the years I've been here," said Paul, who had been Pota's editor on and off for close to forty years. "And I know I could find at least a dozen others if I wanted to look. But don't let that distract you now. The title's of no importance at this point. The story is."

"No, the title is not important now. And I'm glad you said that. But I had a couple of others in mind almost as good I was tempted to use. *From Top to Bottom* was one . . ."

"Yes?"

"Please don't interrupt. *From Head to Toe* was another I thought of. How do you like it? Don't interrupt me. From the soul in the head to the sole of the foot." I might do something symbolic with that one."

"That pun?"

"That homonym. I also thought of this one, *A Pain in the Neck.*"

"That sounds like a good one. It just made me laugh."

"That's the one that got me going."

"Why don't you keep it?"

"Because—you'll think I'm silly—*neck* doesn't resonate. It doesn't connote. It has no literary history. Not like *heart* and *breast* and *spleen* or *tongue.* It has no roots in literature. *Throat* comes close, but *neck* just doesn't fit too well into the plan, I'm afraid, into the skeleton, the body of the structure."

"What skeleton? What body? What structure? Eugene Pota, what are you talking about?"

"I was afraid you'd ask that. The plan, the structure I want to build. Look, I'm trying to tell you. What I have in mind is a novel organized on a biological map, a geography of the human body, sort of. Okay? With each section or chapter corresponding to an individual part of the human form. Like it or not, that's what it is."

"Male, or female?"

"Please don't interrupt, for a while at least. I'm trying to illuminate an idea. Male, of course, with maybe a few digressions to the female, maybe for comedy, for risqué comedy. Now here's how it goes, will go. It's very much like what Joyce does with Dublin in *Ulysses.* Remember? Except that I cover the human form instead. Mainly the exterior. Get it?"

"Are you joking?"

"Are you being funny? No, I'm not joking."

"The way I remember it, Joyce doesn't set out to cover that much of the city of Dublin, not the whole city. He's in there, and that's about it."

"Well, I think you're wrong, but I'm going to cover the structure, most of it, anyway, of the form of the human body. From top to bottom, from the soul in the head to the sole at the bottom of the foot. There'll be a foot in the door at the end, modulated by the lurking danger of an Achilles' heel, if I want an unhappy ending, or an Achilles' heel followed by a foot in the door, if I want to close on an optimistic note for the human animal, and humanity itself. How do you like it so far now? I'm going to use our human form as a blueprint in much the same way that Joyce used *The Odyssey*. That's why I used the word *skeleton* before."

"Are you crazy?"

"No. Do you think so? Why do you ask?"

"Well, you've surprised me before. So maybe you're not. The way I see it, if Joyce had not been telling people all those years about *The Odyssey* as a foundation, no one would have guessed it was there. All it does is impose a snobbish mystique and help justify the inclusion of a number of sections that would be incomprehensible and not worth bothering about otherwise, and still are."

"Where did you get that idea?" coldly asked Pota.

"From you," answered Paul. "You said that exact thing in a book review a number of years ago. Didn't you?"

"Yes. Yes, I guess I did. I didn't think you would remember, or that anyone else would."

"And what is your plot, your subject, what is your story?"

"I was worried you would ask that. I don't have it yet. But

that would be secondary. The subject of this novel, like Joyce's *Ulysses*, would be the novel itself."

"Secondary, eh? Who is it about, who are your people?"

"I'll work that out later. It won't be hard."

"The way I remember it, in Joyce, Leopold Bloom had a son who died, a father who committed suicide, a daughter who's turning into a slut, if there still is any such thing, and a wife who comes three times that same afternoon with Blazes Boylan tickling her from behind. Now that's all pretty meaty stuff. None of that is in the original Homer. And then there are things going on with that Stephen Dedalus too, who pales somewhat in the memory, but he's there also. What have you got?"

"Why are you carping about it now so much?"

"Why are you telling me and asking me? Isn't that what you want from me?"

"I can match dead children and suicides easily, maybe even echo those same ones in a literary way," said Pota. "That shouldn't be hard."

"And meanwhile?"

"Meanwhile? Meanwhile, I'm not sure."

"Then meanwhile," offered Paul, "I've got something new to tell you that you may or may not like. I'll be retiring at the end of the year. I'll be out of here."

Oh, shit, thought Pota. "Now you too? Paul, what's doing it? Cancer, Parkinson's, congestive heart failure?"

"Nothing like those," answered Paul. "I should have said, I am being retired. You're not the only one who's gotten old, you know."

"How did they ever find out about you?"

"They looked at my paycheck. I've been here a long time.

They did some simple arithmetic and saw they could hire fifty or sixty young people just out of college for what they're paying me."

"Doesn't the quality make a difference to them?"

"Not anymore, I think. Not to the people up there at the top now. A cog on a wheel is just like any other cog on the wheel. Who else is out? You hinted at someone else."

"Aaah," Pota groaned. "My Swedish publisher sold his company to a larger one and now seems pretty much out of it, although he tries to pretend he isn't. My editor in Denmark was made to retire because of his age. In Holland, the Dutch one moved from a large company to a smaller one, and I'd be surprised if it was entirely voluntary. All of these have been friends. In Italy, Count Bompiani is dead, and I don't know who's there who cares about me anymore. And in France, they think I'm one of the best American authors of European novels. But American authors of European novels don't sell especially well there, and they seem to have grown tired of publishing me at a loss. And just about all my doctors are gone now too, and I don't know how to go about finding new ones as good."

"A generation cometh, Gene, and another generation passes away. But the news is not all bad. I'm comfortable with a very good pension and retirement plan. And I'm going to be on retainer here to edit all the books I've signed up before the end of the year and all the other books they get that nobody else wants to edit. So if you'll just shake a leg in the next few months and send in something I can buy and offer a contract on, we can stay together until death do us part."

"You don't want my pain in the neck?"

"Give me more."

"I don't have more."

"Get more. Of that one or something else you're genuinely serious about. Give me a chapter or two of forty or fifty pages of something, of anything decent, and something of an outline I can describe at my editorial meetings and in a contract."

"Okay, I've already got one for you, another one, maybe a better one. I've got lots of ideas."

"Too many. You used to do better when you had no ideas and had to find only one to struggle with."

"Hear this one," said Pota, "with a happy ending and lots of war and sex and family quarrels. Now, listen. Try not to say anything until I'm finished. You might like it."

"I like it very much so far."

"There's this good-looking, innocent young man very far back in time—let's call him a prince—and he's sauntering down along a road just minding his own business. And without planning anything, he comes upon these three women not young, not old, but of a kind of ageless and arresting extraordinary attractiveness, larger and more natural than life. He senses something special about them but doesn't know what it is. They beckon to him and ask a favor. What they want from him is a surprise. They want him to judge which one of the three is the most beautiful."

"Oh, shit," said Paul.

"What'd you say?"

"I said nothing."

"I thought I heard something. Just please keep listening."

"But I've heard this one before. Isn't his name Paris? Isn't he from Troy?"

"You haven't heard it the way I'm thinking of telling it. Although, his name is Paris. This is *The Iliad* told from the point of view of the Trojans. Paris is innocent, damn it, isn't he? That's the way the real story begins. He doesn't go out looking for a woman—those three female goddesses stop him. Mine will be a warmer story told from the inside, maybe less a work of literary art, but if so, a story that might be more interesting to moviemakers or even as a TV miniseries or soap opera. Don't you want to see me famous again? No, I'm not kidding and I'm not crazy either. Now, here goes. 'Pick me,' one of them whispers, taking him aside, 'and I'll make you great among all men.' That one is the goddess Hera."

"No kidding."

"As God is my judge. A second one, seeing this going on, takes him aside and says into his ear, 'Pick me, and I'll make you a hero in war. Don't listen to her.' And the third—"

"Aphrodite, of course. That cunt, as you called her."

"Of course. 'Pick me,' the cunt says, arching her back and turning slightly to present to him under her robe a callipygous formation more perfect than ever he has seen or pictured in his life, 'and I will give you the most beautiful woman on earth as your wife.' 'You?' he inquires innocently, for she is good looking. Remember, he is innocent in this version and doesn't even know who he's talking to. 'On earth,' Aphrodite stresses, and he begins to get the idea. Of course, he does what you and I would do. For people like you and me, those other choices aren't much. He picks the most beautiful woman. Now, what he doesn't know—"

"And we do."

"—is that the most beautiful woman on earth, Helen, a

daughter of Zeus, not yet of Troy but still in Sparta, is already the wife of a great Greek king who owns the promise of all the other great kings to rush to his aid with arms if ever anyone should try to interfere with his marriage. And this in due time leads to the Trojan War and all we know about it. But as seen from inside Troy. What we don't know all about is what takes place inside the city from the beginning to the end. But I do, and that's what I'll supply. There's the friction with his brother Hector, of course, with his parents and his other brothers, even before the war starts, and with Helen too, certainly; there's all those acts of combat, as the Trojans see it, and all the rest."

"Where's the happy ending? Didn't you say you had a happy ending?"

"Paris kills that raging dolt Achilles, remember? After Achilles slaughters Hector. With an arrow to the heel with the help of Apollo, who tells him that's the only place Achilles can be wounded. He avenges the death of Hector and all the other Trojans Achilles has dispatched."

"And then," said Paul, "Troy falls, the city is put to the torch, all the men and male children are put to death, and all of the women are taken into slavery. Some happy ending, not even for the Greeks."

"I'll stop long before then. Paris and Helen get together again and make love at least one more time. The eventual tragedy of defeat is something we all know about and will add to the irony of the celebration, the unspoken irony in our knowledge of what is to come. What do you say? Isn't that worth a contract?"

"Is it something you really want to commit yourself to doing?"

"I don't know."

"Then I don't know. Try writing it up with a chapter or two and we'll see how we both feel about it."

"You don't sound overwhelmed."

"And neither do you. I've been around too long to be overwhelmed by anything that isn't already completed. But I'd rather have you rewrite *The Iliad* than *Tom Sawyer*."

"There's something good in that Tom Sawyer idea."

"But you haven't found it yet, have you? Find it and we'll see. How is Polly these days? Your Polly, not Aunt Polly. Has she gotten over your idea of writing a sex book about your wife or some other woman you make up? How's she taking this restless slump of yours?"

"Polly's okay. You know that. And she'd be happier if I settled down and went to work on something. She says I'm easier to live with when I'm wrapped up in something."

"I'd be happier too and so would you. What ever did happen to that sex book you were thinking of? You had a good salable idea in that title. Did Polly object?"

"Not really. Not strongly, as long as it was clear it was not about her."

"Exactly. But who would be able to tell?"

"Exactly. That's what she's probably been thinking too. And me also. Polly is plump. I can make my woman slender. Polly is short and dark. I can make mine tall and blonde. Polly's from Nebraska, I can make my heroine from the South."

"And no one would ever guess."

"Everyone would guess. But I haven't given it up. What I really want to do, you've known, is write another really good novel that will be a big best-seller and a natural for the movies."

"Gene, I think those days of big best-sellers are already long in the past for both of us. Unless you really want to try to write a book with lots of—"

"I don't. And I probably would not be able to if I tried. But I've got these notes and bits of research for the sex book we both might adore. Let me ask you something. Paul, did you ever hear of a diary quotation by the duchess of Marlborough in which she says, 'Last night my Lord returned from the wars and pleasured me twice with his boots on'?"

"Of course. Why?"

"I've been trying to track it down and can't find it anywhere. I think I might want to use it. I've even asked a historian friend of mine who's also heard it but isn't sure where to find it either. Although I'm not sure he's looked."

"Well, if you can't find it, and he can't find it, hardly anyone else will be able to find it either. So do what you want with it. If the truth comes out from some invidious scholar, the publicity will be good for us. So do what you want with it, do whatever you want with it, whatever seems best."

"Exactly," said Pota, and decided he would.

A SEXUAL BIOGRAPHY
OF MY WIFE

by

Eugene Pota

"Last night my Lord returned from the wars and pleasured me thrice with his boots on."

Duchess of Marlborough

A SEXUAL BIOGRAPHY
OF MY WIFE

A New Novel

by

Eugene Pota

CHAPTER 1

"Last night my Lord returned from the wars and pleasured me thrice with his boots on."

I did no such thing.

What the hell is the matter with that wife of mine, anyway, putting such things into a diary and leaving it opened to that page for me to find? resentfully protested the middle-aged author (wrote Pota), intent on starting and completing a contemporary sex novel from the point of view of a modern woman with the captivating title of *A Sexual Biography of My Wife*. His name was Lloyd ———. He was not a lord, her lord or anybody else's. He had not returned from any wars but had been home nights more or less consistently now for several months. He owned no boots. And if there's a woman anywhere in the world I would try to pleasure thrice these days, he muttered aloud, and try unsuccessfully, he conceded inwardly, it certainly is not going to be the woman I've been married to for nearly twenty-five years. And maybe that was precisely the reason she was indulging herself in such extravagant illusions these days. Perhaps. Perhaps? But perhaps they were not fantasies.

That his slender, blonde, Southern-born wife was crazy was no secret to him, crazy in the normal way common to many of today's wives as described continually, almost without exception, by the devoted husbands who spoke also of them with some tolerating affection. That she impulsively and erratically kept a diary or journal—neither of them was sure of the difference any longer, and with her tendency to ramble about anything in mind when writing, as when speaking, it made no difference. That she neatly scribbled into it whatever thoughts were hers at that moment—activities, actions, plans, along with any quotations she judged so apt that she might wish to repeat someday—was also known to him. But that she peppered and sweetened her entries with erotic fantasies of the kind he had just accidently come upon was to him a shocking disclosure.

He returned to the dresser drawer upstairs in their bedroom to look again and assure himself that he had not been dreaming. He saw it was a brand-new ledger that lay on top of her slips and panties. The pages were all blank except for that solitary entry. What the hell did it all mean?

The thought struck him that if it was not a mere idle reverie it might be something cunningly entered in code. Not about him but about someone else. He felt hurt by that thought, scorned—deceived too, but that seemed to be the least of it. In abject resignation he began to examine his memory. He'd been home every evening and night. But often he'd gone into the city and spent long days away, and she'd known beforehand he would be gone. And often too she had gone into the city alone, more often than he; and often as well, she had spent nights there alone, she said, in the small apartment they kept there, she said. Was it possible? The woman writing she'd been pleasured three times was not the amiable, proper housewife he knew. But was it possible she was a different and more treacherous woman than the house-wife he thought he knew? And where could she find a man, or a boy, who would pleasure her thrice? And where the hell had she found such a word as *thrice?* Was it possible there was more than one man, or boy, in action with her?

Lloyd was aware, pervertedly aware, that his spirits were rising with hopefulness as his thoughts advanced along this degrading course. Here, of course, was grist for his mill as an author, a secret treasure trove of authentic female sexual ma-terial for the sex novel he had set himself to write. But some-thing additional was causing him to smile optimistically. Could it possibly be that his serenely contented wife of al-most twenty-five years was secretly a concupiscent babe with very hot pants, pants hotter than he knew? If so, and she be-gan to look better to him with the thought, it could happen that he would begin enjoying her more ravenously too, as though she were the ravishing wife of someone else, and maybe even want to strain himself to succeed in pleasuring her thrice too, or kill himself trying.

As an American novelist, Lloyd ———— had been moder-ately successful and fairly widely known for almost all his adult life, and at present—

And at present, Oh shit, groaned Pota, and stretched out

his arms and rolled his head about to relieve the stiffness in his shoulders and the pain in his neck. He did indeed again have a pain in his neck. But there did not yet seem much he could do with that. About this guy Lloyd ———, would he really have to go again into all this pedestrian background material about him? Maybe he could leave almost all of it out of this novel if it all proved extraneous to his plot material. Or wait till later to worry about putting it in until something more than obligatory exposition occurred to him for integrating it humorously and actively into his spirited sensual subject matter. He skipped ahead on his lined yellow pad to something he already had in mind and already knew he wanted very much to include.

....

And he had Lloyd, fuming, demand:

"What the hell's the idea?"

"What idea, darling?"

"Mildred, you know what idea. Leaving that book right out there for me to see."

"What book? What are you talking about? Lloyd, what the devil's gotten into you this time?"

"Your diary, that's what I'm talking about. Right out there and opened, for me to see."

"Oh, that. Now it's my turn to get angry. I didn't leave it out there in the open. I don't like the thought of your prying into it. It was in the drawer with my lingerie."

"Right there on top, dammit. And the drawer was partly open. And you know how I feel about your lingerie. I couldn't help reading it. What the hell is going on?"

"It's a note in my new private diary, and nothing's going on. Why are you shouting? What are you in such a snit about?"

"I'm not in a snit. I'm in a rage. But I'm shouting very calmly. Just what the hell do you know about the duchess of Marlborough?"

"Who?"

"Marlborough. The duchess of Marlborough."

"Nothing at all. I've never heard of her. Why?"

"No? Then where did you get that quotation from her you wrote down? And where the hell did you ever hear of that word *thrice?*"

"From you, dear."

"From me?"

"Yes, yes, yes. I saw it on a sheet of paper you left out on your desk, and I wrote it down. I thought it was funny. That's what gave me the idea."

"Idea? What idea?"

"For the book."

"Oh, my God. What book?"

"My sex book."

"What sex book?"

"For writing a sex book, a novel, from the point of view of a woman who still enjoys making love. I think readers today are ready and will respond to something like that."

Lloyd ——— sat down, his brain reeling, and paused a moment, inhaling deeply, to recover his wits and think. "And what makes you believe, how do you know, that the duchess of Marlborough still enjoyed making love? When you say you never even heard of her."

"I've really never heard of her, have no idea who she was, or is. But she uses the word *pleasured* to describe the action. And she doesn't seem annoyed that her husband did it to her three times, without even wanting to waste time taking his boots off. I think a woman like that might be an interesting character in a novel I might write. Don't you?"

"And a novel? You? You're thinking of writing a novel?"

"Look how many other women are writing novels. Why shouldn't I at least try? I'm thinking of something that would be seen as a kind of sexual autobiography."

"You've never written anything longer than a baking column for the local newspaper. And where did you ever get such a crazy idea?"

"From you?"

"Again from me?"

"Yes. Aren't you writing a book now called *A Sexual Biography of My Wife?*"

"You know I am, you know damn well I am."

"Well, then what's so crazy about it? Why can't I write one too?"

"At the same time? The same book?"

"It wouldn't be the same book. And why not, if it keeps me busy? Maybe we can publish them together."

"No, Mildred, we cannot publish them together. We will not publish them together. And where will you get your information? Where do you think you will get your information?"

"Well, I've had some experiences of my own, you know. And I've heard from other women. I did go through high school. And I did go through a coeducational college and live in a coeducational dorm. And . . ."

"And? What are you thinking of next?"

"And I can get stuff from you, if you'll let me. From your days in Greenwich Village with all those drug addicts and nymphomaniacs. What was the name of the girlfriend you had for a while who spent months kicking the heroin habit and then was killed in an automobile accident? I left a blank space and I want to put in a name."

"You've started already?"

"Oh, yes, I've got three chapters. And I can get a lot more material I'll need from you if you'll help by letting me read your pages as you write them. Will you let me see them?"

"No, Mildred, I will not let you see them."

"Then I'll make things up. But tell me this much. When a man stands up and finishes urinating, does he always have to wash—"

"His hands!" roared Lloyd ———, in a voice rising to a tormented wail. "Just his hands, if he wants to. He washes just his hands."

"Do you?"

"Oh, God, this is too much! This is mad, Mildred—insane!"

Oh shit, groaned Pota, this is much too maddening and insane for me to keep under control, and already much too complicated to try to keep track of without an outline, let alone for that writer in the book to keep track of without his own outline. Pota saw he would have to stop writing right then and take time to lay out an intricate road map very carefully to try to determine just where and how far he could go with this new turn of events in his plotting.

A walk to the beach would not be of help. He was already much too weary in mind and body for any kind of exertion. Perhaps a nap would have a refreshing effect, he hoped, as he laid himself down. And he gave thanks to his lucky stars that his own wife, Polly, was not thinking seriously and secretly of writing a sex novel or any kind of novel—as far as he knew—or was she?

A development like that one would be just too much for one aging human brain to incorporate without whirling itself away into chaos: he writing his sex novel while his wife also was writing one, and his novel being about a novelist writing a sex novel while his own wife was writing the same or a similar sex novel and trying to steal his ideas.

That would certainly be an unforeseen comic twist, wouldn't it? And he was tempted for a moment to steal upstairs to search through her pads and spiral notebooks to make sure they were not enclosing a sex diary of sorts or a secret manuscript. But he knew she was not. So firmly in place now was the settled contentment between them that no such improbable action could arise to imperil it.

There might be a gold mine in something like that, he thought, but not for him, not now, not anymore.

Oh, God, he exclaimed, and did not care this time whether his entreaty was silent or uttered aloud, where has that beautiful muse of mine gone off to who has been so wonderful to me all these years?

After a minute or two, his answer slipped in on a tangent, laterally, and Pota, rising with a smile, took up his pen.

A SEXUAL BIOGRAPHY
OF MY HUSBAND

by

The Goddess Hera

As Told to

Eugene Pota

A Novel

CHAPTER 1: INTRODUCTION

If I had a friend, I would ask her to collaborate with me in writing a sexual biography of my husband for all the world that comes after us to know the truth about all his bad behavior and all I've had to go through, about all I've had to suffer to preserve our marriage and remain a good protector goddess of the home and the family. Oh, could I write a book about that. But I don't have a friend I can trust. And I can't write. At least I don't think I can. Aphrodite is as close to me as any other woman, but we don't truly like each other, and she doesn't always tell the truth. Not to me, anyway. I've gotten nowhere with her, trying to find out if anything ever happened between her and my husband, Zeus. I know, we all know, that Zeus went chasing madly after her one time long ago. That she was the daughter of Dione, and therefore possibly his own daughter, would have made no difference to him. He's a god, you see, the head god. And thinks he can do whatever he wants to. It did not stop him in the least with Demeter and Persephone, but that's another story I will talk about later in this book of mine that is going to be a very long exposé indeed if I'm going to reveal all of his infidelities I know about, and I don't know the half of them. Zeus could find new women to fall in love with and rape faster than I could uncover and deal with the old ones, to say nothing about the pretty young boy Ganymede, whom I really can't envy yet as a rival, to say nothing of any others like that. But I still can't find out if anything sexual really took place between Zeus and Aphrodite. He won't tell me, of course, and used to get more and more annoyed when I asked, so I've stopped asking, or tried to. And all I get from her are those teasing tosses of the head and suggestive titters.

"You can tell me, Aphrodite," I'd ask. "Now it doesn't matter anymore."

"Oh, yes it does," she'd say with one of her mocking laughs, and give herself a trampy twirl.

Can you imagine?

"It doesn't," I'd promise. "It's all so far in the past it can't matter anymore."

"Is it?"

"I'm merely curious now, after so many others I know about and have been through. It will make no difference."

"Won't it? I think, Hera, I know women much better than you do."

"I swear it won't bother me. I give you my word as a goddess. Did anything ever happen with you and Zeus? I really want to know."

And she answered—you won't believe it—do you know how she answered?

"That's for me to know," she answered, "and for you to find out."

Can you imagine? That shameless cunt.

I'm not a bitter woman, or a mean one. Heaven knows. But I did have to gloat with lots of satisfaction when I saw her weeping so much after that pretty boy Adonis she fell in love with was torn to bits by a wild boar or some other animal. It served her right, I thought. But I'm not a nasty person. Ask anyone. Anyone but Zeus. He can't be fair.

Zeus swallowed his first wife, you know, swallowed her whole, alive. I am not his first. He swallowed Metis alive when he learned she was pregnant and was afraid she might bear a son who'd prove more powerful than he was. My husband comes from an unbroken line of powerful men who swallowed all their male children, or tried to, in fear that one of them would grow strong enough to overthrow them. It must be in the genes. We have them too, you know. It did not seem to occur to any of those thickheaded brains of theirs that if they had not been so threatening to their sons, their sons might have had no reason to overthrow them. Metis was gone, but their daughter survived. And Zeus had to have his forehead split open with an axe in order for Athena to emerge full-grown from inside him. He had a very bad headache for a while and was much more careful after that.

My colleague Athena is therefore the daughter of another rival of mine. We get along pretty well, I guess, but I never forget that she is the daughter of a woman who was with Zeus before I was, of a woman I have to think of as a rival, even though she was there in the past. You would certainly do the same, wouldn't you? Wouldn't you do the same?

It took up much of my time to get even, not with Zeus, who was untouchable, but with his women and sometimes their offspring. Getting even with Heracles for his mother, Alcmene, took a lifetime, his. After he strangled those two serpents I sneaked into his crib to kill him, I knew he was charmed—another damned demigod, like that drunken Dionysus, another bastard son of my husband's. But I bided my time and kept after Heracles constantly. And when the hour was right and everyone was off guard, I drove him crazy and in his fit of madness saw him kill his wife and his children under the delusion they were his enemies. That's how I finally got even. Would anyone blame me?

And that woman Io took a long time too; she was very hard work. To begin with, Zeus turned Io into a cow to prevent me from killing her. That seemed all right with me—being turned into a heifer seemed punishment enough for having been overpowered by him. But then I remembered his other girlfriend Europa and that Zeus had no trouble turning himself into a bull to get to her. Hmmm, I thought. I wasn't born yesterday. He thinks I was born yesterday, turning her into a cow. So I set Argus and his thousand eyes to stand guard over her and make sure they did not come together again. But when Argus was turned by Hermes into a peacock and his thousand eyes into a peacock's tail, I decided it was all not worth the effort. So I set a gadfly upon Io who stung her and stung her wherever she went and drove her out of the land and up into Ionia and down into Egypt, I think, and that's pretty much the last I heard of her, although some people here think she was worshiped there as the goddess Isis. I couldn't care less, as long as she'd paid the price. I'd had my revenge, although I am not a vengeful person. And no one would blame me for taking my revenge against a woman who'd attracted my husband and allowed him to rape her.

But these were mortals. It was with the immortal women that I had the most trouble. I could not kill them; I could not do much to their children, who were immortal too. With Leto I found a way. I put the fear of god, of the great goddess Hera, into the people of every land into which she wandered during her pregnancy. None would face my wrath, and none would let her stop there, none but a place called Delos, which rose up as an island after she bore there the twin children Apollo and Artemis, who are now still up here with me. Of course, we have never been close. Artemis, who would rather hunt than do anything else, is chaste and fancied Hippolytus, who also was chaste and resisted the advances of his stepmother; Apollo, our sun god, so to speak, is not chaste. On the contrary. He "chased" Daphne right into a laurel tree, and he killed the girl Coronis in a fit of jealousy after hearing she'd been unfaithful to him. Then he changed the bird that told him, the crow, from white to black for having told him. Apollo and Artemis both, like Hermes, being children of Zeus, favored Troy in the great war that eventually broke out. Dardanus, who was the ancestor of the kings of Troy, was the son of Zeus and another of my rivals, Electra, that daughter of Atlas, and that was another reason I did not like the Trojans and the city of Troy. I had more reasons too. Paris was there, whom I'd not forgotten or forgiven, and soon Helen was there too, another offspring of my unfaithful Zeus, the daughter of Leda, whom he'd approached as an innocent swan and then raped as a savage beast. Helen in Troy was unhappy enough without my intervention, disgusted with Paris for his acts of cowardice and threatened with death by her wronged husband, Menelaus, until she blinded him with her bare, beautiful breasts that even Aphrodite envied, and I do too, and he lowered his sword and took her back as his devoted wife. There was still more in Troy. Sarpedon was fighting there, another son by Zeus with another consort of my husband's, Laodamia, and when Patroclus speared him to death in one of the battles there, he did not know that he was sealing his own death warrant. Zeus fell in love with the Nereid Thetis, so did Poseidon, and I grew to like her also, especially after the secret came out from Prometheus that she was fated to bear a son more powerful than his father. After that, they all shied away, and she was married to a mortal and gave birth to the unbeatable warrior Achilles, who became my champion in the war against Troy. While Zeus, of course, was siding with Troy, but in the end, as always, the Fates would decide.

After that, Zeus kept away from the immortals and fell in love, as he put it, only with women on earth. That made it easier for me to avenge my honor and my pride.

Before that there were more than I knew about and more than I could count. I knew about Europa, one of the earliest, whom he tricked in the guise of a lovable white bull. There was Mnemosyne, the mother of the Muses, although I'm not sure Zeus was the father of them all. Aphrodite would know, that goddess of love, but Aphrodite won't tell me. Do you know what she answered when I asked her?

"Ask me no questions," she answered, "and I'll tell you no lies."

How do you like that bitch? Isn't she a bitch?

And then there was Themis, the mother of Prometheus, but also the mother of the Seasons, and it was no secret that Zeus was the father. Maia, another daughter of Atlas, lay down for Zeus and gave birth to Hermes, who, loyal to his father, slaughtered the guard I'd posted to keep watch on Io. And Hermes, by the way, had a son with Aphrodite in another one of her extramarital affairs. Aphrodite was married to one of our children, Hephaestus, and cheated on him all the time, with Ares and all of the others. And of course there was Demeter, that goddess of agriculture and vegetation, who lay down with Zeus and gave him the daughter Persephone, who in turn lay down with Zeus and gave him the son Zagreus. This was much too much for me to bear, and I persuaded the Titans to devour that son. Do you blame me?

Aphrodite always tried to blame me.

"Hera, why do you always carry on that way?" she's chided me more than once. "There's really no reason to get so upset."

"Why?" I've responded. "I'm not only the wronged wife of an unfaithful husband who betrays me. I am the goddess and protector of the home and the family. What will my worshipers think of me if I let all this pass?"

Aphrodite giggled loudly enough for others nearby to turn and hear her ridicule me. "Worshipers? What worshipers? Hera, you have no worshipers. Maybe an old woman here and there or a bitter ugly wife. Nobody worships chastity and fidelity. What fun is there in that? And you were cruel and unfair to Alcmene. She was tricked. She didn't know what she was doing."

"She slept with my husband."

"She thought it was her own husband. He came into the bed disguised as Amphitryon."

"She should have been able to tell the difference. My husband is special. He is Zeus."

"And what could she have done? Fought him off? And do you really expect any mortal woman in her right mind to pass up the chance to mate with Zeus and produce a hero? It's just not fair for you to try to punish Alcmene by trying to murder Heracles in his crib and keeping after him all the time."

"I was not trying to punish *her*," I replied, with great emphasis on the last word. "I was trying to punish Zeus."

"And that wasn't fair either. Why get so angry? Why make yourself so angry over something like that? You know how men are."

And some women too, I thought of replying.

But I don't like to argue. I don't like to make trouble. I try to get along with everyone. Am I wrong? Maybe there was something to be said for Alcmene and Heracles. But Semele was different, and no one can blame me. She knew who he was and she knew what she was doing. So I tricked her into asking Zeus to grant one wish for her before she opened herself to him the next time. "You have not seen him as I have, in all his brilliance. Make him promise to show himself to you that way. And then you'll know how he really looks in all his splendor." She did. He did. And she was burned by the brilliance of his lightning to a crisp in half a second. Zeus, though, took the son she was carrying into his thigh and carried him there until it was time for him to be born. I could see that Dionysus too was charmed. "You leave him alone," Zeus thundered at me in command, and I quailed. "In time he will come up here with the rest of us, and Heracles too."

I gave him my word. But he'd said nothing about any others, and as soon as he had turned his back to go off after somebody else, I went to work on the couple he had left Dionysus with as his guardians. I drove the man mad and he killed his son, I drove the wife mad and she leaped into the sea with their other child. I taught them a lesson they'd never forget. Wasn't that a good lesson?

And while I was occupied doing all this, Zeus was carrying on with Antiope. That's another story to come in full detail later on, how the twin sons she bore Zeus eventually became rulers of the city of Thebes. Zeus has his bastard children just about everywhere, doesn't he? I was too late to do anything about that one, but Antiope paid a painful enough price without me. She fled from her father, was imprisoned by her uncle, and treated most cruelly by her uncle's jealous wife. I am not a spiteful woman, and I did not need to have revenge of my own. It was more than enough just to see her suffer.

I was in time for Callisto, though. Zeus stole up on her disguised as Artemis, whom she trusted. But as soon as he had her off alone, he went right to work and did his business. What I did to Callisto before he could stop me was turn her into a bear. And then sat back and waited and watched to see how he would deal with that one. He never even tried. I brought the son from that one up to be a hunter and then led him to Callisto to kill her without suspecting he was killing his own mother. That would have been a neat one, wouldn't it? But Zeus turned up in time to thwart me. Before the son could spear her, Zeus turned her into stars and flung her up into the sky as a constellation, the constellation Ursa Major.

By then I was tired and ready to give up, to yield to the advice of Aphrodite and let him have his way without upsetting myself too much. I let him carry on with the nymph Aegina,

whom I'll talk about later in this sexual biography of my husband, and did not say a word. I pretended I didn't know. He
came to Danaë in a shower of gold, which I still do find
rather nice and romantic, locked up as she was in a tower
by her father. She gave birth to Perseus, and I was secretly
pleased when, without my doing anything, they were cast
away by her father and nearly killed. And god, the great god
Zeus, only knows how many dozens of others. I kept my
mouth shut with Elare and Echo and Juturna and Lamia, or
tried to, and put up with them, because I had to. I said nothing, almost nothing. There did not seem to be anything else I
could do that I wanted to. I certainly did not want to leave
him and did not plan to. Until one day he came home with
the clap.

In a way that was funny.

But I couldn't laugh. Funny too was that the one person
who might have known how to treat his symptoms, Asclep-
ius, our medical man, had already been killed by him with a
thunderbolt for having restored Hippolytus to life. Others
could laugh, and did, but I couldn't, because they were laughing at me too. And I certainly didn't want that runny big thing
of his stuck inside me again until the disease had passed. So
I left him. Yes, I finally left him. In dead of night I took off
without a word and sped to Boeotia, and in a cave on Mount
Cithaeron I set myself up in a new, separate residence.

And I waited. I could tell what would happen. He would
be furious at finding I had gone, humiliated too. They would
be laughing at him again. First the clap, and now this. He
would soon know where I was hiding and he would hurry to
me to get me back. First he would storm in and rage and
command. I was no longer afraid. Then he would beg. And

with dignity I would say to him that not until he got down on his knees and begged a long time would I even begin to think of forgiving him and returning. And then there were conditions I would set. I made up a list, and he would have to give his oath as a god to always abide by every single one of my terms.

I would show him.

But none of that happened. What he did was unexpected. What he did instead was find another woman, a mortal on earth, and marry her to replace me as a wife. Another wife? Over my dead body, I howled, as soon as I learned about it. I tore out of my cave like a whirlwind and sped directly toward the wedding procession. Nothing would stop me.

And there the two of them were, sitting beside each other so gaily, drawn in a cart brightly decorated with garlands of wreaths and colorful flares of flowers, and people dancing around them. She was perched beside him in a white veil with a tiara of laurel and a lovely wedding gown of purest white. I went right for her. I flew at her face with my nails flashing. I ripped away the veil. With another swipe I slashed off the gown. And then I had to laugh. I laughed and I laughed. Zeus was laughing too. Inside the gown was not a woman but an effigy of wood. That impish devil of a husband of mine had tricked me that way. And he kept on laughing too. We went back together, of course, and have been happily married ever since.

ZEUS

That's what she thought, and still does. I tricked her all right, but not in the way she imagines. With Hera gone, frankly I felt kind of good. There was an easing of tension and a feeling of relaxed relief. And after a little while, the thought struck me that, given my position, it might be smart for me to have a mortal wife on earth who was available to me all the time. And the darling girl Lycra in Boeotia seemed just right. Pretty, soft-spoken, willing to please me and submit, eager to bear my children, and with all the delightful spherical, physical signs of abundant female fertility. We had the big wedding and everything was moving along smoothly on schedule. And then came Hera.

I heard the hurricane roar of the wind before I caught sight of the furious flash of her form. Oh, God, I thought, with typical husbandly terror. Her teeth were bared, her eyes were fiery, her arms were raised for battle, and her pointed long fingernails were aimed at Lycra like vicious lances. I re-

acted in seconds, and I am still proud of the marvelous ingenuity with which I performed in this crisis of surprise. In less
than an instant I got rid of Lycra. I replaced that sweet one
with a wooden effigy, turned her into stars, and deftly flung
her into the skies as another constellation.

Hera didn't suspect, and I still see her every night.

"Are you absolutely sure," asked Paul, "that you do want to write a sex novel at this stage of your career?"

"Should I be?"

"What do you think?"

"What do *you* think?"

"That much is up to you."

"You're my editor," snapped Pota. "I want your suggestions. It's why I come into the city to see you. I think I detected a shadow of doubt in your question."

"Do you really want to? That's about the only thing that counts. You're an original, Gene. I can't have any idea of what you have in mind until I see some of it."

"Well, Paul, I'll confess. I'd sure like to do a book with a good chance for a movie sale."

"We don't do things for that."

"We sure do want it to happen, though."

"We don't say so."

"And," sighed Pota, "I'm not even sure I can. The last time I tried I found myself transferring from a sexual biography of my wife into a sexual history of Zeus and then, without knowing why, almost into the closing pages of *The Iliad* with the death of Hector and the tears of his father."

"Those are interesting transitions. I'd love to see how you made them."

"I'm never going to show you."

"You serious guys always seem to have lots of trouble with plots, don't you?"

"Yes. We do. Not always. But by now I think I've really grown to hate plots. I don't much like action. It interferes with serious thought, ideas."

"And ideas interfere with action. It's one of the big differences between our American and your European novels. But in that case, what kind of movie do you think could be made from any new book of yours? Still photographs, album portraits? Tell me this," continued Paul. "It puzzles me. A bit. Are you sure you aren't reacting nervously out of habit, the more so because I'll soon be leaving?"

"What are you talking about?" asked Pota.

"Why are you so determined to keep on writing anything at all? When you don't have to. Force of habit?"

"I have," confessed Pota, meekly, once more, "nothing else to do. The phone isn't ringing much anymore with calls I don't want to receive. There are no faxes coming in with requests for interviews I don't want to give, no invitations from people I don't want to see for parties I don't want to go to. Damn it, I miss those interruptions! Some days the phone doesn't ring at all! By now I think writing is about the only way I can define myself. I won't know who I am or what I'm doing with my life any longer if I'm not working on a book."

"And why do you persist in going so preposterously far afield for subject matter? To gods, to myths, the Bible, to the fictions of other authors. All of them far-fetched novelties."

"Novelties?"

"Yes. Wouldn't you say so? You want to be serious and you keep fooling around with outlandish ideas that don't go far enough. Why don't you write about real people again? About yourself?"

"Paul, real people are not impressive anymore. Or even convincing. We're trite, overdone. So are you. And everything realistic I think of writing about I feel I've written before, or am in the process of reading by somebody else. And . . ."

"And?"

"And, as I said, I want to keep writing because I have nothing else to fill my time with that's fun."

"Fun? Ha, ha."

"Ha, ha, yes. I could nap more and go brooding about aimlessly more. But that's not much fun."

"I nap and brood a lot too. But that's what comes with lasting so long, Gene. It's another one of the prices we have to pay for keeping alive. Please don't think I'm lighthearted about being forced to retire."

"But at least you will still have work to do to keep you busy."

"Yes. Working on books I think much of and probably assigned to a good many I won't. Why don't you and Polly travel more? It's what we try to do when I have the chance."

"To where?" said Pota with a sneer. "I hope I never have to

set foot in another museum or cathedral again. I've already been to the Villa d'Este in Como, the Quisisana in Capri, and the Sirenuse in Positano. The only places left in the world I might want to travel to are back to the Villa d'Este, Capri, and Positano, to sun myself and look at all the pretty ladies. Have you begun to notice yet, Paul, how many lovely women there are these days, now that we've grown too old to bond properly with them?"

"My concentration has been fixed on other places. It's a pity, Gene, you didn't make your money on Wall Street. Then you could play golf, collect art, buy houses, and smoke and talk about fine cigars. And the money you made on Wall Street."

"Thank you."

"So you might as well write another book."

"Thank you again."

"And do it fast. You know we'll probably publish it. No matter how weak it turns out. It would not destroy you, not forever."

"With that I have to agree. And if it did destroy me forever, it would only destroy me forever for a month or two."

"While you're back sunning yourself in Capri or at Villa d'Este and eyeing all the lovely ladies."

Pota sighed loudly. "It's hard work, and a losing game in the long run, isn't it? A reckless career at best. You should have heard that speech I made a little while ago."

And Pota wondered again, as he had long before written in one of his magazine pieces, where James Joyce could possibly have gone after *Finnegans Wake*. Proust, that lucky asthmatic, he reflected now, was another who was fortunate enough to die before being compelled to face that awesome choice.

"How," Paul inquired hesitantly, as though making a reluctant decision, "are you and Polly getting along these days? All okay?"

"Fine," answered Pota with surprise. "I pay the bills, she runs the house. Neither one of us wants surprises. There's ecstasy in the bedroom each time I open a dresser drawer and see the laundry's been done again. Why?"

Paul was smiling too. "That's too bad."

"Why's that?"

"But save that line. Just a thought. I had a sudden feeling there might be a very good novel hidden in a marriage something like yours, an older writer and his wife, told from your point of view and hers, the writer's and the wife's, in alternating chapters. What do you think?"

"I think it stinks," said Pota immediately. "And I've already written books about marriage, more than once."

"Then do another one," Paul argued in a raised voice. "For godsakes, hundreds of other novelists are writing books about marriages, even while we sit here talking and wasting time. It wouldn't be the same one, would it? What's the matter with some of you people? Why must every new book be a completely different one?"

"It's how I am, I guess," Pota murmured, sheepishly. "It's the way we are."

"Then," said Paul, hesitating again, but this time dramatically, "I have another good idea for you, maybe even a better one. Why don't you do what you've been doing and talking to me about for almost a whole year? Although you don't seem to realize it."

"What's that?"

"Why don't you write a portrait of the artist as an old man?"

"What?"

"Don't get angry. You've even got the right name for it. Pota, a perfect acronym. Portrait . . . of . . . the . . . artist. *P-O-T-A.* I can already see the book jacket and the catalogue copy." Paul lifted his eyes reflectively and made a frame of his hands. *"Portrait of the Artist, as an Old Man."* He looked down and cringed away with a start from the searing glare focused on him. "Or . . . ," he hastened to add.

"Or?"

"Or, maybe also on the title page, as a subtitle, an alternate, *Or, A Sexual Biography of My Wife.* That way we can suck in an extra, unsuspecting audience who will think it's your intimate pornographic sex book. Maybe we can even get that Hollywood sale you want so much—"

"And you do too."

"—before they've read it. Why not try writing that one?"

"And why," said Pota, "don't you just go fuck yourself again?"

"You said you wanted my suggestions."

"I don't want your suggestions," asserted Pota with a feigned air of disgust. "No matter what I said. And you know it. I want praise, only praise. Do you think I'm any different from the rest of us? I'll tell you what I really want, Paul. I've been almost too embarrassed to say it even to myself. I want to cap my career with a masterpiece of some kind, a great, original work, even a great very small one. I want to crown my end with applause, to go out on a note of triumph. Like an athlete dying young, but my race finally run."

"And who doesn't? I'd like to do that with you too."

"And," said Pota, "I think I can start out with a half dozen better ideas than that thing you just came up with."

"Can you? Good. Are you sure? Yes? Good again. I'm glad to hear that. Then go ahead and pick one to concentrate on. What the devil are you waiting for? At least give it a try."

Pota listened well. "Paul, I think I will!" he vowed, with a resurgence of optimism he had not truly enjoyed in months, his confidence whetted by the hopeful excitement in Paul's challenge. He came to his feet with spirit, as though excavated at long last from a muddy quagmire in which he had been stuck too long. "Why not?" he continued. "I have to. I promise I will. And I'm going to come up with something different, you'll see, something serious and entirely new. And I'll probably have an outline of something fresh and original, and fifty pages or so for you in a couple of weeks, the way I used to, in the old days. My mind is buzzing already, the creative juices are gushing again." Grinning, Pota raced on with accelerating enthusiasm. "Probably I'll have most of it all worked out in my head by the time I get off the bus back home. I'm thinking already."

"Fine. We've still got the time."

"I will."

"I'll wait."

"You'll see."

"Tom?"
No answer.

Oh, shit, sighed the elderly author, and chuckled to himself once more.

He was not surprised, and he began to think seriously of writing the book you've just read.

The End

About the Author

Joseph Heller was born in 1923, in the New York City borough of Brooklyn. Drawing on his own experiences during World War II, he wrote the novel *Catch-22*, published in 1961. An eventual international bestseller, with millions of copies in print, the book was made into a film in 1970. Heller wrote several subsequent novels—*Something Happened, God Knows, Picture This,* and *Closing Time*—as well as two works of nonfiction, *No Laughing Matter* (with Speed Vogel) and *Now and Then,* and a play, *We Bombed in New Haven,* which was produced on Broadway. Heller died in December 1999.